Suzonne of Twin Flames

Volume 1 of 7 - Chapters 1-10

By Janie Lynn Peterson

SUZONNE OF TWIN FLAMES - VOLUME 1 OF 7 - CHAPTERS 1-10

First edition. March 23, 2023.

Copyright © 2023 Janie Lynn Peterson.

ISBN: 979-8215936863

Written by Janie Lynn Peterson.

Table of Contents

Series Introduction:
A Hint of the Story to Come

Suzonne was born in 1784 on the French island of Martinique. The land is a lover of the wind where the air has the scent of sugar and vanilla. Suzonne and her older brother Raphael inherit the family sugar plantation; Twin Flames. When a hurricane assaults the island in 1799 Raphael's young son, Charles, is gravely injured. There is no way to summon help. Suzonne must call upon the healing skills she learned from many hours in the slave quarter, a place her parents forbid her to go when they were alive. She worked alongside her wise slave Rutah stitching together bleeding slaves, healing snake bites, and acting as a midwife. Earlier Rutah has a vision which predicted a great evil coming to Martinique. Suzonne believed the hurricane to be that evil until shocking events soon proved otherwise.

Suzonne is coming of age. Beautiful, spirited and courageous; she must fight her way through a terrorizing path of evil voodoo and a family history she knows nothing about. When her brother turns to alcohol, Suzonne turns even more to Rutah and giant Tumba, the slaves she has known all her life. The townspeople gossip about her but she does not care.

Suzonne is pursued by a French Marquis and a wealthy English aristocrat. Both are dangerous. Can either of them gain her trust?

Though most of her contemporaries are betrothed or married, she has not made that a priority until now.

While Suzonne never believed she would see a real pirate in her lifetime, she will see many and violently encounter one in particular. She does not consider herself capable of taking a human life but she will commit murder without hesitation.

Suzonne of Twin Flames is a tropical saga of historical fiction laced with adventure and the supernatural of voodoo. It is rich with vivid scenes and captivating characters interacting in a memorizing story that has a way of staying with you.

Chapter 1:
The Hurricane

High atop the cliff, Tumba folded his prayer rug just as a violent gust of wind heavy with sand and surf, slapped him to the ground. He fell backward and realized this was not the usual tropical storm they had expected. This storm, only minutes before landfall, had developed into an unmistakable brutal hurricane.

"Hurricane! Hurricane!" the powerful slave shouted, though no one heard him over the storm's thunderous wrath. He dodged debris as he ran from the cliff house toward the plantation. The storm flag he had hoisted was beginning to shred, its mahogany pole trembling violently. Everyone knew a storm was coming but only Tumba saw the tell-tale gale force winds slam twenty-foot waves on to the beach below. Larger, more ominous waves spiked further out to sea, hurling toward the island of Martinique.

Silhouetted against a churning sky, Tumba fought to maintain his footing down the mountainous path. His bare feet slipped on the loose wet stone but he caught himself. He must warn the plantation to take shelter! Missiles of torn palm and stinging beach grass assailed his body. He allowed nothing to stop him. Three years ago two slaves died in a hurricane that came in like a tropical rain storm that soon became lethal. Tumba harbored guilt. If only he had known what to look for then.

He approached field slaves cutting what sugar cane might be salvaged before the storm. "Hurricane!" he roared! His deep voice commanded their attention. They dropped their machetes and ran through the torrents of rain that followed Tumba toward the fortress-like refinery.

Tumba continued warning everyone he saw until he located his master, Raphael, who struggled to secure the stable ... alone. The frightened stable slaves had scattered and were cowering in their hiding places. Tumba's blue-black chest heaved with exertion. "Bad hurricane come," he panted. "I tell field boys run to refinery."

"Well done Tumba. How much time do we have?

"It come fast."

"Bring anything you can lift into the stable; tools, tack ... even that small trough can do damage if tossed about. Then, I need you to corral some stock near the barn."

"Yes, mastah." He submissively obeyed though the towering, broad-shouldered, barrel-chested slave dwarfed all other men. Even the tall, muscular Raphael appeared diminutive beside Tumba.

The two men worked in unison protecting as much property as their strength allowed. Both were drenched, their clothing becoming heavy and cold, their faces shiny with rain. The pelting deluge mixed with escalating winds made it so difficult to see that Raphael said, "Go home Tumba to your family."

"Yes mastah."

Hurricanes were deadly. They had the ability to destroy a plantation. Every planter built a wind house for his family. Wind houses were made of stone with walls well over three feet thick. In areas with greater storm vulnerability, the walls could be five feet thick. When Raphael's first child was born, he built his family home and his own wind house leaving his father and sister to remain in the original fortified house which his father had incorporated into a large manor. Raphael chose to build his wind house into the side of the cliff that separated the plantation from the ocean. Wind houses were not meant to be lived in, as they had few amenities. They were used only during severe storms.

Earlier that evening, Raphael had battened down the wind house where his wife Adeline and their two sons were huddled. Now there was trouble. Their eldest son Charles had gone missing!

"How did you lose Charles?" cried Raphael.

Adeline sobbed, "I did not lose Charles. You know he despises confinement. He begged to see the storm. I granted him permission to step outside for the count of ten and not one second more. When I called for him, he didn't answer. The wind became so violent I struggled to open the door. Charles had disappeared into the blackness!" she wailed.

Raphael turned on his heel back into the storm.

Nine year old Charles was a wayward boy given to adventure. He caused his father much distress. Raphael searched for the boy yelling his name. He prayed he could be heard over the roaring hurricane now that the cries of the slaves had subsided as they found shelter. He climbed the stairs outside the refinery leading to the bell tower. Punishing winds challenged him all the way. He tripped, cut his shin, continuing with resolve, he clutched the rails.

Twin Flames Plantation was nestled well behind high cliffs but its property extended to include a strategic lookout point overlooking the ocean. As a result, they were often first to receive a hurricane's initial blow. They strongly felt it their responsibility to sound the warning bell. This time, as Raphael pulled the ropes, he prayed not only to warn the island but bring his son to safety. The bell rang out like a whiney ill omen distorted by the wind. "Charles! Charles, come to the refinery!" he shouted in between clangs. "Charles! Charles! Where are you?"

Raphael's fifteen year old sister Suzonne did not hear her brother's cries but she heard the bell. She knew what it meant. The worst kind of storm was here building strength and it would be vicious. The words her slave Rutah uttered in a trance two days ago, burned in her mind.

"Bones say a great evil come," she had chanted, "Bones say it be true. No mercy." Her dark fingers lightly touched a myriad of sun-bleached bones she laid out in a pattern.

"What kind of evil Rutah? Is it here now? Is it a plague or another war? Tell me Rutah pleeeze!" But Rutah had only moaned … "No mercy." Her head fell back and her amber eyes rolled so aggressively they seemed to disappear into her dark molasses colored forehead. She raised her head.

Suzonne saw her dull glassy stare. "Rutah, you'll need your rest now." She had been a witness many times and knew what followed Rutah's spirit dream time. Suzonne rose to leave the hut. "Rutah, before you sleep, I must go through the door. Will you release the spiders?"

Rutah waved her arm in the direction of the thick silken spider webs that protected her threshold and she drew a symbol in the air.

Suzonne watched the huge, hairy brown arachnids scurry to the sidelines allowing a brief opportunity for her to pass through the door. She closed her eyes and covered her mouth before she slowly walked out sideways. They did not upset her as long as none of the web touched her mouth. She could never tolerate that! Not unlike an army of precision soldiers, the spiders moved to enclose the opening minutes after Suzonne exited.

This process never ceased to fascinate Suzonne. It became one more thing she kept secret from her family and friends with regard to Rutah.

Suzonne had not connected Rutah's ominous warning with the storm expected before sunrise. She prepared as always. Martinique had many rain storms. She addressed the family friend who acted as her house man. "Milo, we need to bring in the canary cages from the veranda and the Italian statuary from the courtyard. We'll place them in the welcoming vestibule as always." She knew the walls there were five feet thick. It had been the plantation's original safe house.

Suzonne threw a light fishing net over her mother's cherished orchids as her father had always done. She stood still and sniffed the air. Something had shifted. The usual sugar scented breezes were replaced with the salty-fishy scent of an angry sea. She cringed with foreboding. "Milo, I fear this is no ordinary storm. See how the wind increases?" She pointed to the bending palms that encircled the manor. "Are the shutters secured?"

"Yes, every one."

"We don't know how long the storm will rage on. We'll need food and water." Suzonne and Milo hurried to the citrus grove where Lutesse, the cookhouse slave and her daughter Fancy joined them. Fancy nervously tugged at her braids, entwined with a brilliant red jasmine flowering vine.

With the escalating winds whipping all around them, they harvested two large baskets of ripened fruit. Suzonne knew her brother, Raphael, would not be pleased to see her working alongside the slaves.

"You don't work with the slaves," he had scolded, "you tell them what you desire. Then, you must firmly see that your wishes are carried out."

Suzonne found it difficult to be stern with them. She had lost her mother when a young child and these slaves had been her caregivers for most of her life.

"Lutesse, take the fruit to the cookhouse while Milo and I get fresh water." Suzonne's slight frame was ill-suited to work the cistern, but Milo was not a young man. She had learned to ease it open using all her weight moving the pulleys while cranking the handle with her foot. Milo positioned the bucket. "There," she said well-pleased to see a steady stream of fresh rainwater began flowing into the bucket.

The ferocious storm pounded the roof. Palms were now being forced to the ground!

"Rutah warned me about this storm! She called it evil!" Suzonne clutched her father's crucifix which hung about her neck along with a voodoo charm from Rutah.

Suzonne learned to respect black magic. She had seen many things in the slave quarters, a place her parents had forbidden her to go. For her, there had never been fear because she had faith in Rutah.

Rutah knew the sex of every baby before its birth as well as what their fortunes would be. Adolescent girls often consulted Rutah for information concerning their matrimonial futures.

An Obeah woman named, Euphemie David, told Rose Tasher of Trois-Ilets across the way that she would one day be the Empress of France. Rutah had smiled in agreement and the same day, Rutah added that Rose was to marry a man named Napoleon who would change her name from Rose to Josephine. As outrageous as some people believed the predictions were, Suzonne never doubted that her slave had been right.

The marriage took place in Paris on the very date Rutah had given. Suzonne had to hold her tongue when she encountered those unkind people who made fun of Rutah and herself. Instead, she had derived tremendous satisfaction by grinning a very naughty extra large grin at the person whenever the subject came up in conversation which happened quite often.

The royal reign had not yet come to pass however; Napoleon Bonaparte was now a beloved and powerful general as well as an astute politician in France. Suzonne fully expected Martinique's Rose to ascend the throne one day soon with her new name, Josephine.

A wind surge jolted Suzonne from her thoughts ripping off roof tiles and crashing them to the court yard floor! Sabre, her elderly dog yelped and ran from his hiding place to his beloved mistress. He cocked his head, then, moved from her embrace and crawled toward the fallen tiles, tail down, whimpering.

Suzonne rushed to investigate. She screamed "Charles!" There lay her nephew, unconscious bleeding from a wound on the side of his head.

Chapter 2:
Providence

Charles had been struck by one of the falling roof tiles! Instinctively licking to clean the bleeding gash, Suzonne's dog Sabre was already tending to the boy's head injury.

"Charles!" cried Suzonne, falling to her knees beside the limp boy. "Charles!" He did not respond. "Milo, help me take him inside!" They carried him through the arched garden doors, struggling against the fierce wind. "We'll lay him down on the great table."

The elongated family dining table was the perfect height to perform an examination. Suzonne placed her hand on his heart and counted the beats, all the while comforting him with soothing words. She raised his eyelids, one by one. "Good, unless he begins to vomit, we can be hopeful that his brain has not been affected."

Suzonne cradled Charles' bloody head while Milo fetched water and a bolt of muslin. She gently rolled the boy's body on its side to elevate the injury and position his head facing up.

"Charles, Charles," she spoke softly. "Awaken, all is well. You're with Aunt Suzonne." She held his hand. It was cold but pulsed with life. She drew the ample tablecloth over him when he began to shake and quiver.

Milo brought a bucket of cooled water from deep within the cistern. Suzonne applied cold pressure to the wound. "I must stop this bleeding! If we can keep his body warm and his head cool ... The first blood cleanses but the continued blood loss concerns me. He's too small. I don't know if he's able to replenish it as fast as it's leaving him! I'll need my sewing basket and the honey jar."

Suzonne's knowledge came from hours spent in the slave quarters observing and more recently, assisting Rutah treat the slaves' health issues. Suzonne had attended the glories of birth, the triumph over unspeakable injuries and the devastation of death. Through it all, Rutah remained calmly in charge.

This time the patient is a family member and Suzonne alone must act and make the life-saving decisions. Precious time could be lost delaying treatment to bring Rutah there. Besides, Rutah may be in the midst of crises of her own in the slave quarters due to this dangerous storm.

Suzonne thoroughly cleansed Charles' wound. She knew it was too deep for proper healing and the incessant blood flow that comes from a head wound continued to alarm her. "I call upon every angel and every saint who loves Charles to descend now to help stop this loss of blood and please guide my hands and judgment," she said.

"Milo, I'll require two lamps, one over each shoulder. After we submerge our hands in rum, you must hold the flesh together while I sew it shut," said Suzonne.

"Yes," He answered weakly.

Suzonne glanced up at him. She had never seen him so pale. His tawny complexion was chalky and his lips were very dry. "My God, Milo, I need you! Do not faint. Is it the blood?"

Milo clutched the back of one of the table's chairs. "It is seeing so much blood on a child. It was I who buried my children after pirates ransacked our village."

Suzonne caught her breath. She remembered the story of tragic loss in his Mexican homeland. "I should have remembered. I'm terribly sorry, Milo. I can't imagine the horror you've suffered." She paused. "Though neither of us could save your dear children, I pray that together God will allow us to save this child. I believe he has been thrust into our care for more than the obvious purpose."

Milo nodded. "Yes. We will save Charles." He poured a bottle of rum into a serving bowl reserving a few swallows for himself. He thrust his hands into the brown liquid. He made the sign of the cross. "I am ready."

The first time Suzonne had to pierce flesh with a needle, she nearly lost her courage. She accomplished it under Rutah's tutelage. With her jaw clenched and her lips nervously clamped together, she had somehow persevered. In time, blood was not upsetting to her as long as she saw that the patient was being made better.

Now, without Rutah, Suzonne monitored the wound. She waited for the bleeding to slow to a clear substance. "Ah, there it is. Now, all three of us are ready." Suzonne plunged her hands into the rum along with the needle and thread. Milo stood beside Charles and followed her instructions. Suzonne worked at the end of the table above Charles' head. She began to pull the thread through with cautious dexterity. Her precise stitches earned a first prize ribbon the last year of school. Sister Mary Evangeline had no idea that her star pupil would one day be sewing together gashes rather than creating fine pieces of lace.

When the wound had been closed, Milo applied honey, a protection from the sickness that brings the deadly fevers.

Charles made a slight movement. His limbs felt chilled. They added a comforter over him to form a second layer. His eyes fluttered while he murmured something inaudible. Suzonne spoke his name. He opened his eyes again, responding to her voice, but appearing dazed. She reassured him of his well-being. "Charles, you've had an accident in the courtyard. Do you remember coming to your Aunt Suzonne's during the hurricane?" Charles stared blankly at her. "You hurt your head but it's much better now."

Milo asked, "Is he able to speak?"

Suzonne said, "He should be able to speak unless he's been weakened by loss of blood. I've done all I know to do. If only one of us could venture out into the storm and bring Rutah to Charles. I'm worried that my judgment may have been lacking or faulty."

Outside, the storm continued to rage. Thunderous banging, breaking and cracking sounds unnerved them as heavy items were flung against the very walls they counted on to keep them safe. How many more years could the old structure hold tight against the pounding of so many hurricanes?

No matter the danger, Suzonne decided she must have Rutah's consul.

"Aunt Suzonne?" Charles moaned.

Her spirits brightened, though clearly the boy suffered with pain. He became agitated crying and, impossible to console. Suzonne could not allow him to further injure his wound with his rolling side to side.

Milo held Charles while Suzonne prepared a lemon tea. She blended it with the compound of herbs Rutah had created for Suzonne's dying father. They contained a potent pain reliever that had helped ease his discomfort and enabled him to sleep. She guessed at the proportion, giving Charles only one-fourth the dosage that had been administered to her father.

Suzonne lingered near him, and eventually, Charles slept a peaceful sleep. His face relaxed and his cheeks regained a trace of color.

Suzonne yearned to close her eyes along with Charles and rest but she continued to feel the need for Rutah's approval. She forced herself to stand and turned to tell Milo. "In spite of the storm I have to bring Rutah to Charles."

The immense entrance doors were thrown open, slamming into the vestibule walls with a crash! An exhausted, battered Raphael entered the dining room. His frantic eyes sought his sister. "I can't find Charles," he cried. At almost the same time he saw the blood stained, unmoving body of his son laying on the table.

"My God, my God, "He's dead!"

Chapter 3:
Rutah

His forlorn words hanging in the air, Raphael looked past Suzonne horrified to see Charles so still and as pale as the linen tablecloth draped around him. Raphael gasped; the boy looked like he had been laid-out for a wake reminiscent of his baby brother, the son the family lost two years ago. "Oh my God!" he screamed. "Has another son been taken from me?"

"No, Rafe ... Charles lives!" Suzonne moved toward him. Raphael pushed her aside. He hunched over the boy crying his name. His over-tasked body buckled under him; he slid to his knees. Charles did not stir. "He's dead! He's dead!" Raphael began shaking the boy's shoulders, lifting him, caressing and kissing him.

Suzonne wrenched her brother's arm back away from his son. "Stop, Rafe. Charles is alive! I give you my word. Lay him down, you're too rough. He doesn't hear you ... he only sleeps. I gave him Rutah's powder. It eased his pain and encouraged this much needed deep sleep."

Looking stunned and confused, Raphael released his grip to lower the boy gently back down onto the table.

"Here," she put her hand on Charles' chest. "Place your ear to his heart."

Raphael complied. "Yes, I hear it," he managed a weak smile. "Thank God," he sighed while searching his sister's eyes. "What happened?"

Suzonne encircled his slack arms with hers and hugged him. "You've had a terrible fright." She turned to Milo who had been standing in the shadows and requested he bring them a flagon of their father's best aged rum and a pitcher of water.

Before the tinkling glassware on Milo's tray could be heard, Suzonne explained how Charles had been found.

Soon, Raphael's relief turned into a frustrated rant. "That boy will bring me to old age." He slumped onto a silk upholstered couch with his drink. "He's been sneaking the new stallion out on moonless nights, riding him with only a bridle. He's been thrown off time after time yet, he returns, determined to break the beast. I now have old Solomon guarding the horse from my own son. His mother has been sickened with worry about him ... now this. I need to alleviate her anxiety that Charles has been found. Milo, has the storm calmed enough to send someone to our safe house and give Adeline the good news?"

"I believe it has calmed. The winds are no longer throwing missiles at the manor. Tell me, what is to be said to her of Charles' injury?"

"Soften it, say only that he has a cut and I'll bring him to her soon after he's awakened from his nap."

"Thank you, Milo." Raphael stood to pour himself another golden drink. This time, he tapped her glass to toast Suzonne's watered down version which was almost gone. "Hmmm, rum, is that a proper beverage for a young lady?"

Suzonne stiffened her posture. "Tonight, I'm not a young lady. I am an aunt and a sister feeling gratitude that we have survived the worst of this hurricane. I'm an aunt and a sister who also needs a bit of rum."

Raphael sat back surprised and somewhat amused. "When did my little sister grow up without my notice?"

She had no reply for that question. "I wasn't going to speak of this with circumstances so recently dire but my drink encourages me. Charles may resemble his mother's family but he's your son, Rafe and he behaves as recklessly as your reputation at that age. When I was nine years old, so ill with that fever, papa entertained me for days with stories about you as a youth. Remember the time you and the Marceau brothers used the property for a race track? He said you pushed those horses so hard between and around all the buildings; the chickens didn't lay for a week. Papa laughed about it when he told me, but I'm certain he throttled you at the time and felt just as you do now about Charles."

Raphael smiled and shrugged his shoulders. "I can't deny it."

Suzonne said "I know your energy, your intelligence as well as your rebellious temper. So, don't wonder at Charles' antics, my dear brother. Instead, look into the mirror."

Raphael's smile faded. "How you sting me with your words. No more drink for you." He placed the flagon high on a shelf.

Their attention quickly shifted to Charles when the boy began to fret and thrash about.

"He's very uncomfortable." said Suzonne. "The pain preparation is wearing thin. It was left from papa and is almost exhausted …"

Raphael cut her off and began pacing, his face grimacing with worry. "Suzonne, thank you for doing what you could for Charles. Now, he needs Dr. Marmont."

"How can he be located in this storm? Please allow me to fetch Rutah for Charles, if only until Dr. Marmont can be reached."

Any dissatisfaction Raphael felt with his son melted as he once again knelt beside him, comforting him with pats on the boy's shoulders and the sound of his voice. "Papa loves you Charles."

Charles's frets became intense moans.

"Adeline and I don't want our son treated by a black magic slave. He deserves better."

"Oh Rafe, who do you think taught me to care for Charles as I have? Now he requires someone more skilled to oversee his condition. Charles needs Rutah!" Suzonne wrung her hands and thought how much she needed Rutah as well. She couldn't live if she harmed her nephew in any way or neglected to administer a treatment that might have minimized his suffering. Out loud, her voice rose with anxiety and asked, "How many of your field slaves has she saved?"

Raphael lashed back. "It's different to be nursed by one's own kind in a familiar manner from your old country. I want my child to be attended by a trained medical doctor not a witch doctor!"

"Papa, help me. It hurts," Charles cried.

Sabre whimpered and whined under the table.

"Can you risk being so particular and stubborn while your son cries out in pain?" Suzonne demanded.

"It was Rutah who made the pain powder for papa. Charles won't need the doctor, but others will."

Drained of energy and too worried to continue, Raphael's broad shoulders slumped. He was desperate and defeated, and he knew it. Even if Dr. Marmont could be found, he might be caring for more severe injuries than Charles, and most likely, hours away. His son needed attention now. With great reluctance, he said, "My argument stands, Suzonne. I only allow Rutah to touch Charles because there's no other solution at the moment."

Raphael collected Rutah himself. He found her with the others in the refinery. She asked to gather a few things from her hut. The slave quarters were in shambles but Rutah's hut and the chapel looked almost untouched.

"Your place held well," he said.

She gave him a knowing half-smile. Her unmistakable hut was larger than the others with a small front porch. Colorful cloth remnants streamed from the rafters. The rough mud walls were stained pale pink with something she grew in one of her miniature gardens and a roughly carved cross hung over the threshold. The most peculiar feature always caused Raphael's skin to crawl. Thick spider webs hugged the perimeter of the entrance and covered her only window. He had seen the large spiders scurry whenever he rode past. He never came closer than the narrow dirt road that ran through the quarter.

"The storm cleaned the webs away." observed Raphael.

Rutah nodded, "Ahuh. They back tomorrow, good an strong, mastah Raphael."

Raphael paid no attention to her reply. He thought about all the years he had seen her working in the slave quarters. He owned her. His father, Etienne bought her in a group of forty seven slaves the same day he bought a herd of livestock. Etienne had not wanted her. She was too thin and he thought odd-looking with her narrow face and yellow-brown eyes. He took her because he wanted her sister, Lutesse, who was said to be a trained kitchen cook slave. To his chagrin, the cook slave had prostrated herself on the ground rolling and screaming to protest the separation from her last relative.

Etienne had many other business dealings that day. With his patience frayed, he threw up his hands, and a deal was struck. As a result, Rutah had been purchased at a fraction of the rest.

The other slaves called her a root-worker and asked to be treated by her. It became common practice to drop off injured and sick slaves at her door. Neither his father nor Raphael stayed to see what she actually did. Anyway, it was just a cultural thing with them, he thought. He was a busy planter, father and husband. He had no time to concern himself with Rutah. What did it matter how she accomplished her healings as long as the slaves she repaired, as he called it, were fit to return to the fields? That had become her value to the plantation. She no longer toiled in the fields.

Raphael's face distorted into a scowl incredulous that this uneducated slave woman would soon be attending his child.

Rutah walked a distance behind her overwrought-master. She wore a large red and white checked kerchief about her head and protected a coarsely woven bag under her apron. Suzonne knew well its contents. She also knew her brother must never see the workings whose ingredients were held within that bag. They had stronger healing properties than herbs and often in a magical way.

Rutah hummed a sing-song melody, closed her eyes and held out her hands while walking closer and closer to Charles. She sensed his energy levels. When she reached him, she examined his wound and drew a circle in the air above it. Then, she looked up at Suzonne with a toothy grin showing her brown gums. "You fix him good, mam'selle. Boy can grow old."

Suzonne breathed a sigh of relief. Nothing meant more to her right now than Rutah's positive critique.

"See trouble here?" Rutah pointed to a faint red line emanating from the center of the wound.

"What you do for boy, stop it."

Rutah touched Charles' forehead. The boy recoiled. She ignored it. "Close eyes and rest. Rutah make medicine, help you."

She sat cross-legged on the floor and pulled a wooden bowl and three pouches from under her apron. She proceeded to crush what resembled dried flowers with a liquid from a gourd. She worked with strong intent until she had created a paste. When the consistency pleased her, she requested a splash of rum in her cupped hands. After blending it between each finger, she rubbed the preparation on a terrified Charles' lips, gradually incorporating it into his mouth. She helped him to drink a cup of water. "Pain go ... see?"

The onlookers were silent. Charles had co-operated with a groggy curiosity while his father did not disguise his skepticism. If she did anything that even resembled what he preserved as devil worship, he planned to call a halt to the whole proceeding.

As if she read his mind, Rutah turned to face him directly. "We fix him mastah, no spirits."

Chapter 4:
Deception?

Suzonne watched Rutah work with awe and admiration. "Rafe, these are ancient healing arts. Don't confuse them with voodoo." Secretly she knew that if the herbs were not enough, Rutah had every intention and Suzonne's blessing to use all facets of her knowledge. But this time her healing preparations were all Rutah needed for Charles.

"Give boy many waters, mastah. Rutah come, more medicine tomorrow. Fix him good."

When the worst of the storm had moved on, Rutah assured the family that Charles was doing well enough to be moved to his own bed. She began to gather her things but abruptly paused. A puzzled expression crossed her face. Turning to Raphael, she asked, "more to fix?"

"More? No, there are no more. No one else needs you."

"Yes," she insisted. "More to fix."

Raphael became agitated. "I said no. There's nothing more for you to do here. Go back to the quarter. Perhaps, it's there you're needed."

Rutah knew what she felt. The need she sensed did not come from the quarter. Someone clinging to life needed her immediately. Rutah was conflicted. Her eyes darted from brother to sister.

Suzonne asked, "Is someone else hurt, Rutah?"

Rutah vigorously moved her head up and down.

"Rafe, is there something you've kept from me? Have we lost slaves?"

"No, Rutah is mistaken. Everyone's exhausted. We need to call an end to this evening. Tomorrow we'll assess the storm's damage in the light of day. We'll need to be rested. I'm taking Charles home to his mother."

Rutah appealed to Suzonne, giving her mistress a penetrating, insistent stare.

Suzonne instantly felt a wave of cold perspiration trickle across her forehead. She trusted Rutah's instincts. "Tell me more Rutah."

"Two need Rutah. They bad hurt."

"Can you take me to them?"

Rutah pushed through the heavy double doors with Suzonne close behind. There stood Raphael with his feet firmly planted holding Charles like a new born. His face had darkened with anger. "This is ridiculous, wasted energy. I forbid you to go! The storm is not over. It could strengthen again."

Suzonne looked at him as if he were the ridiculous one. "Did you say forbid? You can't forbid me, I'll soon be sixteen."

"Suzonne," he yelled. "You get back inside now!"

"Don't concern yourself. I'll be careful," she answered with her back to him.

Raphael watched helplessly as the two rain-pelted women disappeared into the night.

Rutah scurried with a determined urgency. Suzonne's longer strides had difficulty keeping up with the much older woman. Rutah's vitality had always been remarkable. Suzonne pushed herself to stay close behind her on the black winding path. The winds whipped graveled volcanic soil and torn foliage at them as they stepped over masses of hurricane strewn debris.

Suzonne thought they were headed for the livestock pens. Could Rutah be sensing injured animals? They climbed over a downed coconut palm. Horses whinnied in the distance. Rutah took the path that forked away from the pens.

Suzonne brushed rain-soaked hair from her eyes. Where was the healer being led? Rutah slowed her pace, then stopped and raised her hands. She's waiting for a sign, thought Suzonne.

Rutah approached the shed where the plantation hung newly butchered meat to cure. "They be there." She pointed to the large pool of fresh red blood streaming from under the door despite the diluting rain.

"There's always blood there from the meat." Suzonne explained. "Could that be what drew you?"

"They inside." said Rutah emphatically." "That blood, man blood."

Suzonne yanked the handle. "It's locked. "We keep it locked. Raphael has the key."

They heard movement coming from inside the shed. Suzonne saw a loose hinge. Rutah handed her a rock. Raphael came up behind them! Suzonne allowed the rock to fall into the brush.

"What were you going to do, break the door down?" he demanded.

"Yes, of course. To save a life, I'll do whatever's necessary."

"It's a pig, Suzonne. The mysterious patient Rutah conjured up … is a pig carcass. Not even Rutah can return it to life." He feigned a laugh.

Again, they heard movement in the shed. Raphael explained, "Just a rat."

Suzonne raised her voice. "Well then, open it; let the rat out!"

"I don't have the key. If I carried all the keys for the plantation I'd be weighted down. Forget this foolish business. We've learned to expect rats. They're just a nuisance. Tumba will take care of it in the morning. Now, I really must insist that both of you go home, out of the remnants of this storm for your own safety. You know the winds are still strong enough to do you damage."

With great reluctance, Suzonne saw that her brother was not going to back down. She avoided looking at Rutah who she knew would be upset. The women left, retracing the route they had taken to get there. At the sight of the fallen tree, Suzonne grabbed Rutah's arm pulling her from the path into the thick palm branches. They silently waited concealed until Raphael passed them and his movements could no longer be heard down the path.

"You've never been wrong. She whispered to the old slave. "I need to know what master Raphael is hiding. Wait here. I'm going to the barn and get old Solomon. He can open the door for us."

She ran cautiously, searching until she found the old blacksmith brushing a horse in the stable. "Why aren't you hiding in the refinery with the others, Solomon?"

"Mam'selle, I hear horse crazy scared. Know how the storm spook horses. I come back an brush um and talk. Horse quiet right down."

"You are very good with horses: it's as if you know what they're thinking."

"Mam'selle, not safe out in the storm."

"I need to get something from the meat shed. When you make a lock you keep the master copy of the key don't you?"

"Yes, mam'selle. I get for you." He brought her a tin box. "This for shed." He handed her a key with a red string.

Suzonne thanked him and ran back to Rutah. She hoped the noise they heard was only a rat. The rain diminished as they made their way back to the shed. Suzonne stifled a gasp. Raphael stood there with his back to them. He had never left. Who, then, had passed them in the darkness?

The door stood open! Raphael had the key all the time. To her horror, he dragged out a body, leaving it lay slumped on the rain-soaked ground. Next, he pulled out a tall negro boy who cowered in his grasp.

Suzonne rushed at her brother. "What is this, Rafe?" she yelled.

"You just don't give up. I tried to spare you, Suzonne."

"Spare me? You lied to me! Who are these boys? What's wrong with that one?"

Rutah, down on her knees, examined the comatose boy. She felt his wrist; held her hands over his head. When she placed her fingers carefully about his throat, she looked up at Raphael. "Too late. Boy's blood gone. Rutah not fix him." She transferred her attention to the other male whose back had been deeply streaked with whip lacerations.

Filled with disgust, Suzonne yelled, "You had every opportunity to tell me the truth. Rutah might have saved that boy, eased both their suffering. Where's your honor? What is the truth?"

"Truth? I don't know the truth. This boy can't speak French. I'm guessing they're new at the DeLisle Plantation. I found them hiding in our barn when I searched for Charles. Honor? What honor is there in a hurricane? I fended off limbs and branches looking for my son trying to stay alive myself. I could ill afford concern for two runaway slaves."

Rutah's patient shook with fear. She spoke to him in a language close enough to his own that they were able to have a disjointed dialog. "Boy say bad man use him scare angry slaves. Man have black snake. Boys run. Bad man shoot boy. Boy carry hurt boy here."

"What does he mean about a black snake?" asked Suzonne.

Rutah turned the boy around for her mistress to see his back. "Ohhh ...," she winced. "The black snake is a whip! I know of no planter who uses a whip around here. Rutah, ask him where he came from."

The boy answered Rutah by pointing in the direction of the DeLisle plantation.

"I did hear pistol shots." said Raphael. "I guessed they came from DeLisle, someone after these two."

"Didn't you see their wounds?" lamented Suzonne.

"I saw some blood but I thought they hurt themselves running-off."

"Rafe, he bled to death! Rutah might have saved him!"

Raphael threw his arms up in the air. "No more questions, no more judgment. Who are you, Saint Suzonne? You have time for all these virtuous pursuits now. When you are a parent and assume more of the responsibilities on this plantation, we can speak again more equally on this matter. I'll send word to Claude DeLisle tomorrow that I'm holding his runaways for him to pickup. They shot that one; they can bury him. They've already caused me time and needless scrutiny. Meanwhile, I'm going to chain this live one in the barn for old Solomon to look after. He can treat those lash cuts the same way he doctors horses when they're injured."

Raphael addressed his sister's forlorn face, "for God's sake Suzonne, they're just field slaves. They don't belong to Twin Flames. It's not our loss." He slid a rope through the boy's iron wrist cuff and led him away.

Suzonne felt sorry for the boys. They were no older than herself and since when did Claude DeLisle resort to severe lashings to control his slaves?

Tormented Rutah could say nothing. She could do nothing, at least not openly, not yet. She had felt it creeping slowly, steadily ... now the evil had become stronger. It had been hiding but it would show itself soon. Before long, she would know in whom the evil dwelled. It would have a name.

Chapter 5:
Clouds of Smoke

Raphael kicked at everything in his way as he returned Charles to Adeline. The very idea that Suzonne questioned his management decisions and defied him so blatantly infuriated him. She had seldom taken any interest in the running of Twin Flames. Now that she was maturing, he feared her out-spoken personality, would continue to be in his way until she married and left to be with her husband. Until then, he refused to allow her to interfere with his plans.

Suzonne and Rutah trudged away from the shed in silence. The attempted rescue had ended in tragedy. She felt both bewildered and disappointed by her brother's callous behavior. Raphael appeared to care little that his sister had lost respect for him and he cared nothing that Rutah had as well. He ignored their father's steadfast principle: the most productive slaves have more respect than fear for their masters.

Worse, Raphael lied and then gave such a weak explanation for his despicable actions.

Suzonne could not abide injustice or an unnecessary mystery. No matter how she reviewed the evening, it made no sense. "Unless ... Raphael shot the boy. Oh, hideous thought!" She gasped holding her hand over her mouth. "No." She felt ashamed to even consider her brother capable of anything so dreadful. Yet, something was being kept from her. Why?

The storm had been vicious. Suzonne felt grateful to be home again in the manor house with gentle Milo. His calming voice soothed her. "Suzonne, we may rest our nerves. I have walked throughout the manor and saw no severe damage."

"Thanks be to God's heavenly saints," said Suzonne.

She longed to speak to Milo about Raphael and discuss the horrifying incident at the shed. She decided it would be wrong to burden the sweet, elderly man. He looked so tired. Instead, she thought to speak to her dearest friend, Camille, tomorrow at the Delisle plantation. She trusted Camille with her life. Camille always listened carefully and did her utmost to sort out the details of any problem. She had a way of telling Suzonne that she was making more of a situation than necessary without making her friend feel foolish or extreme.

Milo called for the young house slave, Jerome, to mop the vestibule floor where rain water had seeped in from under the great doors. Milo had been meticulously training the fresh-faced Jerome whose pleasing personality and quick mind had qualified him to become Milo's assistant one day.

Jerome burst into the room making more noise than Milo thought necessary. "Remember you are in the welcoming room of the manor house, not the cookhouse or the barn."

Suzonne could not help but suppress a giggle as Jerome's mop playfully splashed the tiled goldfish motif floor. He created an illusion that the fish were swimming for Suzonne's amusement.

"No more foolishness," Milo reprimanded. Jerome's grin vanished at the sound of Milo's crisp single clap together with his raised voice, "Jerome!"

The boy loved and respected his mentor and quickly became dutiful, finishing the job as he should have before being dismissed.

Milo's Mayan features softened when he looked at those he loved. He always looked at Suzonne that way and now she saw how much Jerome meant to him. Her father said that Milo would always be his most trusted and loyal friend. They met long before her birth. Suzonne knew only that Milo had escaped from enslavement in Mexico. Her father, Etienne, had made certain that Milo could never be classified or mistaken for a slave again. He penned a "Free Man" document to that effect, witnessed by fellow planters. Though free, Milo had elected to serve the family by managing their household. "A life must have purpose," he explained. "This work is what I know. Yes, in Mexico I had been forced to do these tasks. Now, it is my choice; my honor. I will stay until I am led elsewhere."

Milo and Etienne, touched by this moment and how far they had come, embraced. Only they and one other knew the extent of the dangers they had faced together as younger men.

"You are weary Suzonne. I am weary. Let us retire for a time. We can do nothing more tonight." Milo followed her outside. They slowly walked through the littered court yard carefully stepping over shards of broken pottery and pools of standing water. An antique blue cloisonné urn had toppled and cracked.

Sabre, crippled by arthritis, lumbered behind Suzonne. "Oh, beautiful friend, I have neglected you today. Forgive me. You are the better friend. You have never neglected me." She bent down to kiss the top of his head. The wind continued to assault the ornamental foliage.

Milo kept watch as Suzonne negotiated the slippery terracotta stairway to her apartments. Sabre struggled valiantly with each step a painful challenge for him. Despite his advanced age he would have lunged into action to protect her if need be. He had been trained to watch over small Suzonne while her mother was otherwise involved in household duties. He had pulled her from a watering trough, barked for help when she fell from her tree house and fought countless snakes in her behalf. He would not leave her side except for the one place he was not allowed to go. She never took him to the slave quarters. He had accompanied her there once but he barked incessantly, ignoring Suzonne's commands to stop.

Rutah simply said, "Dog see spirits. Never stop. He go home."

Thereafter, Sabre walked with her to the lane leading to the quarter. "Sit, Sabre." She crossed her arms at the wrists. "Sabre, you stay." He waited for her like a stone statue hoping that every sound he heard might be Suzonne returning to him. He could not be coaxed from his post no matter how much time passed without her.

Sabre groaned with each step. "Milo, Sabre suffers so up the stairs."

"I know his pain. Rutah can do for him as she did for me. Alas, I too am an old dog." Suzonne smiled, "Thank you. Once again, you have relieved my mind. If Rutah can restore only a small portion of his youth, Sabre's energies would be renewed."

Good night, Milo."

"Good night, Suzonne." Only when he made certain of her safety, did Milo begin walking to his quarters nearer the cookhouse.

Suzonne surveyed her bed chamber. It looked unharmed except for several missing slats from one shutter. She made the sign of the cross. "We are thankful, Father." She sat on the bed's edge and slipped out of her shoes. Sabre plunked down at her feet leaning into her legs pushing to be as close as possible. He nuzzled her. She hugged him and massaged the back of his ears and his neck. "We've survived another hurricane, beautiful friend. Were you frightened? We were all frightened. Milo believes Rutah can help you feel better. I'm so encouraged. I'll speak to her as my first duty tomorrow."

Suzonne La Fontaine was a fortunate mix of ancestry. She had her father's abundant, wavy hair; a rich chestnut with strands of auburn, and glints of gold, the result of time spent in the sun without her bonnet. Under long heavy lashes, her large eyes drew one in only to discover no discernible color. Sometimes they looked green, no blue, or perhaps hazel. They were as blended as her hair, changing with the light, the color of her dress or the room; mesmerizing. She bore her mother's striking bone structure; a strong, but delicate chin, and the prominently placed high cheek bones envied by everyone who did not have them. Like her mother, she had perfectly shaped dark brows. Her friend, Camille had once accused her of enhancing them with an ink-dipped quill.

Suzonne knew the lantern flames had been extinguished. Every hurricane had done so. The lanterns were important to her father. They stood atop black wrought iron gates on either side of the property's entrance. The gates were only locked at dusk which came early on Martinique; about the same time as the evening meal. Simultaneously, the torches were relit if necessary. Her father had been adamant. The name, Twin Flames was scripted to exacting specifications on the gates. "The flames must never be allowed to go out!" he had ordered.

Suzonne acknowledged her fatigue. She slid out from her long damp day dress, leaving it lay where it fell, a small rumpled mound. Nude and shivering, she slipped beneath the lacy coverlet made from her christening garments. Her stomach cramped when her thoughts returned to Raphael and his lies. She had asked him directly and he chose to lie. He said he had wanted to spare her. The Raphael she thought she knew would have told her about the runaways. She rolled to her side as if that would help her think of something else. "Papa, I promise to light the lanterns tomorrow," she murmured before falling deeply asleep.

Suzonne slept fitfully. Not only uneasy about Raphael, her thoughts regarding Rutah's prophesy before the storm haunted her. "Bones say a great evil come ... no mercy." She feared that Rutah's message referred to more than just the hurricane.

In the blackness of pre-dawn, Raphael was awakened by the Marceau brothers; Jacques and Phillip from Chapel Grove plantation. "Raphael!" they shouted while one brother pounded the door with his fist, the other slammed the forged knocker again and again. "Fire at Delisle!"

Raphael opened the door wearing only half buttoned trousers. An undressed Adeline peered behind a tall curio tousled and horrified. "Delisle is burning?" said Raphael with alarm.

"Yes, we're on our way. Get ready."

"Good God! I'll be right out."

"We'll have old Solomon saddle your horse, said Jacques.

Phillip added, "Make certain you are well armed, it looks bad and you know the unrest in their slave quarter."

Raphael hurriedly dressed and ran to the stable. Old Solomon held the reins of his black stallion, Night Hawk. Before mounting, he loaded his pistol and slid a long blade into a sheath on his hip. "We're going to need help." The men rode to Tumba's hut. Raphael bent from his saddle to hit the door with his riding crop. Tumba's woman opened the door halfway. "Tumba gone."

"Shit!" Raphael was more than irritated. "Did he go to the cliff?"

"Prayer time," she answered timidly.

Raphael knew Tumba was a devout Muslim. "Damn it, he's always praying the hour I need him."

"Why the hell do you tolerate it?" hissed Jacques.

"Tumba is the best I have. He's worth more than ten of my other slaves." Raphael looked toward the cliff.

"There's no time," yelled Phillip. He pointed to the sky, growing darker and more menacing over the Delisle plantation. The threesome sped toward the ominous unknown praying that it not be as horrific as it appeared. The closer they traveled, the more smoke stung their eyes and irritated their throats. In spite of the feed sacks they had thrown over the horse's heads, the animals had to be whipped as they faltered against the wind carrying the ever stronger fumes. Jacques' mount rebelled against the whip, pawing the road and refused to go forward. The horse pranced in a circle, vigorously shaking his head to dislodge the bit, rearing up while Jacques battled for control.

When the other horses reacted similarly, Phillip coughed through the kerchief over his nose and mouth, "we have to walk them."

Beyond the choking black air, they saw it; the oldest, most lavish manor house on the island fully engulfed in a ball of fire with spires of flames licking the sky. The ballroom and public rooms had already been ravaged and were smoking, twinkling orange embers of destruction.

Phillip winced, "Mother of God!"

Jacques, the youngest Marceau brother, cried, "Why is no one fighting the blaze?"

Raphael's chest tightened. He shook his head. "There's no saving it." He could hear the voice of his father. 'One day son, I pray you marry Laurette Delisle and we will own this property and create a dynasty. Connecting our families and our land with theirs makes good sense. One enhances the other.

The men tied their horses upwind in a mango grove and slowly approached the fire. They pressed their handkerchiefs tightly over their noses and scanned the ruins of the once exquisite home all had envied. The intense heat kept them back. Tears of disbelief burned down their heated cheeks. They shielded their eyes searching and hoping to see some sign of life when Phillip pointed, "over there."

Two figures could be seen curled together under the canopy of a young royal palm tree. The trio of men ran to them. Camille and her mother sat soot-smudged and hollow-eyed in night clothes. Fiery beams crashed down, then sizzled on smoldering timbers across the formal gardens. The men jumped but the traumatized women sat with an unnatural deadpan stillness. Camille recognized Raphael.

"Raphael, we're all that remains. Papa and Laurette are lost and mama, well ... we are merely holding on to one another."

Raphael, down on his knees, put his arms around both of them. "I'm so terribly sorry." He paused, "Are either of you injured?"

Camille shook her head and said, "I'm too miserable, I can't feel my body. Look at mama. Her hair and night dress are singed and I think her mind is as well. She hasn't spoken one word since I found her."

"Can you tell us what happened?"

Camille attempted to stand, but needed help. "The storm tore at the roof. Pieces of tile fell to the ground. The veranda doors were blown open. I saw the draperies swing wildly. Somehow the lamps were knocked over. I don't know; it all happened in a moment. Laurette and I did our best to smother the flames with a tapestry but it, too, ignited. The wind carried the fire everywhere. Laurette's clothing caught fire. She ran outside and she ran and ran. I chased close behind, and I saw the flames devour her. Her beautiful long hair, Raphael, even her hair was burning!"

Camille sobbed while her mother stared wide-eyed. When Camille's shoulders heaved with such intensity that she lost her balance, Raphael held her tightly.

"Laurette ran screaming. She wouldn't stop running. The pain must have been ... oh I can't imagine. I could do nothing. I wanted to end her misery. If I had a pistol I would have killed my own sister!" Camille took a breath and swallowed. "When Laurette stopped running, she collapsed and died. I poured water on her anyway. Steam came from her body. I swooned and became ill." Camille pointed to a smoldering blackened clump near a rose trellis. Raphael moved closer and saw the charred remains of Camille's sister. He gagged. He had known her all her life. Their family had attempted to pair them but as they matured, it became clear to Raphael that he considered her a dear friend, not a possible wife.

He stood there transfixed at the horror before him and he could only think of the time he got in trouble for coaxing her to race with him on her new pony. He wanted to remember good things about Laurette, not things about himself, but Raphael struggled. He clenched his jaw and forced himself to draw upon all his memories of her even if they were bittersweet.

With his eyes closed he pictured the way she had looked at their last Christmas ball together. They danced under the brilliant crystal chandeliers here in the Delisle ballroom. The orchestra had come a long way and cost a great deal of money. Their parents were beaming at them, already planning an extravagant wedding. Raphael had begun to feel trapped. He remembered the devastating look of anguish on Laurette's face as well as the entire family when he brought Adeline home. Laurette never married and now to suffer this ending to the life of this sweet young lady. How grossly undeserved!

Jacques stepped forward. "Philip has gone to survey the property. How can I be of help?"

Raphael shrugged his shoulders. "It would appear we are too late for Laurette and the manor. Camille do you know the fate of your father?"

In a barely audible voice she said, "I never saw him leave the manor."

Madame Delisle witnessed it all. She had run outside when the draperies caught fire, but returned into the roaring blaze to save her husband, Claude. She saw him taking down an heirloom family portrait. He ignored her pleas to escape and follow her outside. He believed the painting was priceless and that he had time to get it. He did not understand the nature of the home's construction.

The way the fire started had weakened the beams. Claude Delisle's fate had been sealed. A fiery collapsing wall consumed him. The deafening crash drowned out his wife's shrieks. She had been nearer the door and did not share his fate. Madame Delisle was to suffer a death of another kind.

When she entered the garden, Laurette ran past her, lit with flames like a human torch. She saw Camille's valiant efforts to save Laurette. She heard their cries and Laurette's screams as she burned to death!

Madame Delisle watched the fire destroy the home her grandparents had required five years to build. In mere hours she lost her husband, eldest daughter and all traces of their family's history. Her mind could take no more. She wandered until she tired and sat under the palm where Camille found her.

Phillip, on horseback joined them. "I've ridden about the property to evaluate the damage. Although the grand manor and a few adjacent small buildings burned to the ground, the refinery, barns, stable and slave quarters were unharmed." He took Raphael aside. "I know this is not the proper time but Madame Delisle and Camille may be encouraged to learn the estate is more than salvageable. With help from us and others ..."

Raphael interrupted him. "You're right. They have no heart for such thoughts now. They have suffered too much. When the ashes have cooled, we have the gruesome task of searching for Claude's body."

Male slaves began to mill about the grounds. Phillip became uneasy. "Keeping order will be a serious responsibility." He asked Camille, "Where is your overseer?"

"Derk? Drunk, most likely," she said shivering. "That disgusting Dutchman."

"Never mind," said Raphael. "I'll deal with him later. More importantly, we need to prepare a wagon so Madame can lie down. Camille, you and your mother need fresh clothes and a place to stay. Come to Twin Flames. Stay in our guest house for as long as you wish. Suzonne will want to care for you."

Camille, clinging to her mother, nodded. "Thank you."

Jacques covered Laurette's body with a horse blanket he found in the stable while Phillip and Raphael got a wagon and harnessed a team. Phillip volunteered to accompany the women to Twin Flames.

On the way, the women understandably made no attempt at conversation. Phillip decided to take the opportunity to say something he had always meant to say before now. "Your great manor will live forever in the minds of those of us who enjoyed countless balls, picnics and holiday celebrations on the beautifully landscaped lawns and in your lavishly appointed rooms. I referred to it as the Versailles of Martinique. I personally will treasure my gracious wedding held there. Laurette supervised the hanging of orchid garlands in the great hall and the gleaming silver place settings made my wife very proud to have our ceremony in such a perfect setting." He looked to Camille for a response. Her lips were quivering. She made no attempt to brush away the torrents of tears streaking down her soot-smudged cheeks.

"Oh God, forgive a fool. I should have known that my memories have only magnified your losses. I'll say no more. Please accept my apology."

After Raphael waved goodbye to Camille, he asked Jacques to stand guard at the slave quarters' gate. Then, he marched directly to Derk's cottage behind the stable. He flung open the door without knocking. He found the fleshy brute of a man sleeping off a binge. His wife and children were in their cookhouse. Raphael walked through several empty rum bottles strewn on the floor to get to him. He kicked a stool out from under Derk's feet! The man jolted awake. Seeing Raphael, he moved to stand but fell to the floor when Raphael's fist cracked him across the face, blood splattering in all directions.

"You, drunken ignorant bastard. You murdered those good people with that fire!"

"I dought yah wanted dah land!" he yelped in a heavy Dutch accent.

Chapter 6:
Dangerous Discovery

Suzonne dreamed vividly about her father. In the dream Etienne appeared quite young, attractive and healthy. She saw herself in the dream as well; very small, not more than four years old running through the courtyard to a troubled Etienne. He bent down to receive his daughter, encircling his arms around her lifting her high in the air. Suzonne felt the strength of their relationship and the feeling of being protected. Once again wrapped in the luxury of her father's unlimited love, she said, "Papa, I need you to protect me." She pulled back to indulge herself in his adoring gaze.

Etienne's eyes were dark with worry. "Caution, Suzonne, caution," he said all the while his image continued to fade away.

"Papa!"

The dream startled Suzonne awake. She sat up, shaken and forlorn and whispered, "Papa."

Sabre wagged good morning. She heard the clatter of horses and a wagon on the crushed shell, tabby drive. She realized that Sabre's hearing had deteriorated more than she knew. He had heard nothing. He would no longer be able to alert her to visitors. She called his name. He did not come to her. Sabre was deaf. He sniffed the air and became agitated. "I smell it too," Suzonne said, alarmed at the faint scent of smoke; not the smoke from the smoke house or from old Solomon's forging furnace. "Only a burning building smells like that!"

She ran to the window, squinting to identify the dark forms in the early light. The driver looked like Phillip Marceau and she thought she recognized her dear friend, Camille Delisle. "Yes, it is Camille. Something must be wrong!"

Her first reaction to grab the bed coverlet, draw it around her body and race to the vestibule changed when she saw herself in the long mirror. She realized the coverlet was far too revealing. She flung it aside and slipped into a dressing gown and house shoes. She took the upstairs corridor past her father's apartments. It would be faster than going through the courtyard. She opened the great doors before Phillip pulled the bell cord.

"I'm saddened to tell you that Delisle has burned to the ground," he said in a raspy voice.

Suzonne felt her breath being sucked away to the point of choking. She looked out toward the wagon.

Phillip continued, "Laurette has perished. Claude has not been found and is feared dead."

Suzonne rushed past Phillip and ran to the wagon. Throwing her arms around her life-long friend she wailed, "Camille, how can this be?"

"Suzonne", was the only word Camille managed to say clearly. She writhed in agony her tears pouring down tracks of endless tears shed this catastrophic day. Suzonne held her close; unconcerned that she too would now be smudged with soot.

They clung together with Suzonne uttering condolences and prayers. "May God in heaven give Camille and her mother your strength to persevere. We ask that you lessen their pain and help me understand why this tragedy befell her family. Thank you for your guidance in all things. Camille, I mourn with you and the holy saints mourn with you."

She looked to also comfort Camille's mother but quickly saw that Madame Delisle did not appear to be herself. "We must attend to her Camille. Is she able to walk?"

"Yes, if she's led," Camille answered through spasms of anguish.

Phillip lifted Madame Delisle from the wagon. She groaned but had no other reaction to him or to her daughter. Suzonne spoke directly to her, making close eye contact. "Come, Madame Delisle (she had always addressed her formerly). Give me your hand." The traumatized woman extended her limp hand. "You are in a weakened state. Please, don't stand. Phillip, will you carry Madame to our guest house porch? Sit there Madame with Camille and rest until all is made ready for you.

"Milo, our good friends will be staying with us. We must prepare the guest house. Madame Delisle is not able to climb the staircase in the manor."

A flurry of activity bustled about the forlorn Delisle woman. Milo sent Jerome for blankets and placed one around the older lady's shoulders first and then Camille's. He called for fresh linens. Lutesse's daughter, Fancy, arrived within minutes, her braids decorated with a bright red vine dangling almost to her shoulders; she carried a stack of folded laundry balanced on top of her head.

"Very nice, Fancy," said Milo. "Before you dust and sweep, run and bring back Rutah for the ladies. We have vermin in the cottage."

Phillip inquired if he might be further needed as he felt an urgency to return to the Delisle Plantation. In truth, he thought he had heard musket fire coming from there and he did not want to cause alarm. The others believed it to be thunder.

Suzonne assured him that she had more than enough help with Milo and Jerome. He took a last sweeping look about and felt confident that everything that could be done was in motion. Within minutes, Phillip sped back to the disaster that had become Delisle.

An unoccupied dwelling in Martinique quickly became infested with centipedes, snakes, and spiders. Rutah had command over all things that crept, crawled, flew or made a web. Milo had seen her work this magic countless times. It looked effortless, as if anyone could do it.

Rutah circled the cottage while repeating what she called the prayer of her ancestors. One shake with a collection of spirit-infused charms fastened to the end of a gnarled wand, and she prepared for the finale. The unleashed angels of nine came forth drawn by the utterance of two words under her breath. All the while she glared about daring the creatures to defy her. "Be gone!" She commanded in her deepest voice, and with three loud claps of her hands, it was done. Milo and Fancy had run into the yard, not out of fear, but to see the show.

A mass exodus of every kind of insect, two reptiles, and a parade of centipedes poured from each window. A pit viper with a yellow brown back slithered out the door a mere four inches from Rutah's bare feet. Even though a bite from a viper can be fatal within minutes, she did not flinch. Instead, she gave the snake a look that sent him off faster than anyone had ever seen a snake move.

Madame Delisle seemed unaware of the spectacle taking place around her, but Camille's slack mouth still hung open when Rutah turned to the elder woman without fanfare. "Rutah fix maman ... yes?"

A wide-eyed Fancy stared at the Delisle women covered in soot. Camille sniffled, her cheeks streaked white from streams of tears. Their ragged, singed clothing felt brittle to the touch where they had beat out flames from air-born embers.

Fancy thought the threadbare women smelled like a charcoal stove when food had been burnt black by mistake. She was especially fascinated by Madame Delisle's blank look. She had heard of such a condition. She whispered to Milo. "She white zombie?"

Milo quickly escorted her to the back of the building. "Do not speak foolishness Fancy. These poor women have suffered the loss of family members and their home in a fierce blaze. Hurry your cleaning. Have Lutesse heat bath water and prepare food for them."

"Yes sir, Milo. Here come maman." Lutesse, the manor's cook carried a tray balancing a pitcher of orange juice, two goblets, a plate of golden flat biscuits and a covered dish. Camille hoped it contained marmalade.

Lutesse placed the tray on a table between the unfortunate women. She pulled a steamy wet towel from the covered dish and gently washed both pairs of Delisle hands.

Camille did not know how soiled she was until she saw the blackened towel. The kitchen slave offered her a glass of juice. She eagerly drank it down. Her mother made no move to reach for hers. Camille and Lutesse looked to Rutah for direction.

"Glass to mouth. Empty belly push maman out hiding place."

"Is that where she is Rutah, hiding?" asked Suzonne. "Will she ever come back?"

"Only maman know. Maybe come back. Rutah fix maman strong. Potion not fix soul. Maman see family die."

"Might she sip some juice, Camille?" offered a hovering Suzonne, the strain of concern on her face.

"Here mama," Camille held the goblet to her mother's lips. "Have a little taste of orange juice. It will help you feel better." Her mother turned away. "No, no you really need to drink this. Please try mama." Madame Delisle's expression remained frozen.

"Soft talk," suggested Rutah. "Touch maman."

Camille put down the goblet. She tenderly rubbed her mother's arm and shoulder speaking soft tones of encouragement. "We will be better tomorrow mama. I know we will. All I ask is that you eat and drink something today. It's the little things, now mama. We only have to think about the little things like this tiny biscuit." She opened her mother's clenched fist and closed her fingers around the biscuit. "It smells like home. It tastes so good."

Camille directed her mother's hand to her mouth. She leaned over and bit into the other side of the flaky biscuit, pressing the fragment into her mother's mouth. She knew it would melt on contact. If her mother could swallow, there was hope. "Look everyone, she's chewing!"

"Today, good." Rutah placed her hands over the older lady's head. She feared Madame Delisle had no wish to return to reality and until the woman found a glimmer of hope in her future, all they were able to do was keep her comfortable.

Camille kissed her mother and cried tears of gratitude. "See how big little things can be, mama? I know you're there somewhere. I'm going to continue to speak to you as if you understand. It's as much for me as it is for you."

Tumba had run pell-mell through the property looking for Raphael. His prayer rug rolled in one hand, his other hand waving frantically at anyone he saw. "Mastah Raphael!" Everyone he encountered shook their heads. Finally, he rang the manor bell. Lutesse, told him, "Mam'selle and Milo gone to the guest house."

No one noticed Tumba's large frame fill the door until he said, "Mam'selle?"

"Oh, Tumba, good. I'll need you to lift Madame into her bed soon."

The huge slave gingerly lifted Camille's mother as if she were a ragdoll.

"I'm sorry Tumba, I meant after she had been bathed and ready for bed."

Tumba carefully placed her back in the porch chair.

"Mastah Raphael! Not find him. Not home." His eyes were wild with alarm though no one looked up to see it.

"Raphael has gone to the Delisle plantation. There's been a terrible fire ..."

"Come. You come with Tumba. See bad thing."

"Very well, you can show me but first, I must dress and get fresh clothing for our guests."

"Mam'selle, come now." He saw her dressing gown. "Dress, come with Tumba."

Suzonne was taken aback, never having heard Tumba speak with such assertion. She thought thank God her brother had not witnessed the brazen behavior. Lesser infractions had been cause for harsh discipline. But then she saw the panic dominating Tumba's face and quickly went to change into a day dress before returning to the guest house.

Suzonne kissed Camille's cheek. "Tumba has something urgent to show me. Milo will see to your comfort. I'll return soon. Milo, I didn't take time to select clothing for them. Will you send Lutesse?"

"Mam'selle!" Tumba pushed for her to follow him. She had to alternate walking with running to match his long strides. He walked in the direction of the ocean. The path took them through heavily damaged sugar cane fields, downed palms and pieces of every kind of vegetation. He began running. It was the same route he had taken earlier to sound the storm warning.

"Slow yourself, Tumba," Suzonne panted. "Are you taking me to the sea?"

"Yes, mam'selle."

"What is it? Has a sea creature washed ashore?"

Tumba roughly shook his head. "Come!" He proceeded to follow the path, looking back often, making certain Suzonne followed close behind. His expression frightened her. What could possibly be so dire? She thought. This walk to her father's favorite place usually required an hour. Today, at this fast pace, it would take forty-five minutes.

Tumba began the climb up the rocky trail to the cliff. When Suzonne slipped, he came back down to her and grasped her hand. She dismissed the breach of custom allowing her to be dragged up the steep path to the summit. She paused, grabbed her aching side, in front of the plantation's original structure built near the lookout. Her father used it as his retreat and the place he stored his finest wine, and liquors.

"Mam'selle!" beckoned Tumba standing at the edge of the cliff pointing down at the cove below.

Suzonne reached for her father's spyglass, kept on a hook, as she passed the cliff house door. She joined Tumba. At last, she saw the reason for his insistence. A ship wreck! The beach below littered with bodies and the wreckage of a broken ship's cargo assaulted her eyes! She scrutinized the drifting vessel, listing leeward some one hundred meters from shore. Desperate to determine its status; friend or foe from this vantage point, Suzonne groaned with suspicion. She saw a double masted craft. One mast had been split as if struck by lightning. It had both square as well as fore and aft sails. Some eighty feet long, Suzonne counted at least eight cannon; a brigantine, the chosen combat ship of pirates! It flew no flag, not even a tattered remnant could be seen.

Martinique's ports were busy places of commerce. In times of peace, they supplied necessities to the ships of many countries. All legitimate ships flew the flag of their country of origin. Port masters knew their business and needs long before they docked. It made for an efficient trading experience.

No proper ship on course would have elected to come into this cove. Suzonne knew the French merchant ships whose captains were old friends of her fathers' and she could skillfully identify naval ships as well as countless foreign ships she had seen docked at Fort Royal. This ship was to be feared!

"We'll need to hoist the hostile flag. Suzonne continued to access the scene through the glass for movement. Had the rest of the crew been lost at sea?

Originally, Etienne had flown the French flag atop the cliff. After the British took the island, they insisted he fly the Union Jack. He refused. Instead, he created a Twin Flames flag. The tall pole flew that flag unless there was trouble.

Tumba began to take down the storm-shredded hurricane flag he had hoisted only yesterday. The flags were stored in a nearby shack. If there was disease, as so often followed a brutal storm, they flew the yellow flag. For fire they flew the orange flag. When under siege, they flew the red flag. They had a flag for pirates but in Suzonne's memory, they never needed to fly it.

Tumba's eyes widened when Suzonne handed him the black flag. He had never seen a pirate but the whispered stories about them in the quarter were terrifying. He wondered if they could be worse than the sadistic slave master he had endured before being sold to Twin Flames. He secured the ominous black flag with a double knot.

"Run Tumba to the bell tower and sound the warning!"

He turned to follow her orders. "Mam'selle come?"

"I'll stay. We're the only ones who know about the pirates. This wreck must be monitored."

"Bad men hide." He searched the sea and the high cliffs. "Mam'selle not go; Tumba not go."

"There's nothing here to plunder, save sugar cane. We have no ship to replace theirs. The plantation is well concealed, papa saw to that. They could never climb the steep cliff without the rope. The condition of the ship suggests they all drowned."

In the distance, the bell tower rang one, lone peal. Suzonne and Tumba froze, looking at each other waiting for the usual frantic succession of warning bells. There were none, only the creaking death throes of the doomed ship and the foamy surf below.

Without a word between them, Tumba handed Suzonne the crudely made dagger he carried in a snake skin about his waist. He used it to kill poisonous snakes and the foot-long centipedes that tormented the island. Today, it might be used to protect his mistress from a foe neither had ever known before.

Chapter 7:
The Invasion

Martinique's value was in its sugar crop. The economies of Great Britain and France depended upon it. Many battles had been fought and much blood had been spilled upon the twinkly granules of sweet white "Gold". As a result, the elite of Europe became wealthy while enjoying their confections and tearooms for more than one hundred and fifty years.

Currently held by England, Martinique had been controlled by France when Suzonne's family settled there. No matter the owner, the majority of the population remained French. The British garrison housed in a massive stone fort at Fort Royal protected the island and their own interests.

On the road to Delisle, Phillip Marceau continued to hear musket fire. He soon realized that the disturbance he heard came from across the bay at Fort Royal, not the plantation. He readied his pistol when he saw a wagon of men approaching him. He recognized his overseer, George with two slaves who had gone to Fort Royal early this morning for supplies.

"We had to turn back!" George said breathlessly. "Pirates are attacking the city! Townspeople were running for their lives! They told me the pirates had taken refuge on a moored ship and the soldiers positioned themselves near the wharf to contain them. Everyone is worried that the pirates were turning the ship's cannon to fire on the city. If they can't be stopped, the entire town might be ignited!"

Phillip rode off to give the news to his brother, Jacques, and to Raphael. The closer he came to his destination, the more the acrid-laden air assaulted his nostrils and eyes. It hung like a scorched, rain-soaked blanket suffocating the countryside. Though he had already seen the smoldering ruins of the Delisle plantation, he gasped anew at the enormous destruction and coaxed his ride forward while the wary animal snorted to expel the noxious fumes. He found Jacques busy enforcing order on horseback, in the Delisle slave quarters. It was a serious endeavor as there had been an uprising one year before and no one had forgotten the terror of those days. Claude Delisle had been so traumatized; he traveled to Jamaica to hire a strong, competent overseer well-versed in handling difficult slave issues.

He returned with Derk Vandersort, a surly man with a ruthless reputation for being harsh and unyielding. He had been known to accomplish the tasks at hand no matter the consequences. It mattered not that he worked a slave to death. "Dhat's what dar'er for, yeu know."

No one wanted to waste gun powder on slaves. The leaders of the uprising were hung before Derk arrived but his cruel methods of control soon caused the deaths of more slaves at Delisle. The large, broad shouldered, red-faced Dutchman had come from South Africa. Early on in his career, he had been involved in the slave trade but the stench of the ships was worse than his own. Because he knew agriculture well enough and he had no conscience, he easily evolved into an overseer. He was never seen without a loaded pistol and a menacing black, coiled leather whip, affixed at his waist. The slaves called his whip the black snake.

A woman's wails drew Phillip and Jacques to an over-sized cottage near the out buildings used for food storage. The woman ran out screaming, "he's killin him!"

Earlier, an angry Raphael had split Derk's lip before he began the search to find Claude Delisle or his remains. Raphael prayed against all odds that his old family friend and neighbor had escaped the fire and would miraculously appear, unscathed. When he came upon a singed skeleton wearing a molten ribbon of gold around its neck, he knew the truth. Claude's brother, a bishop, had given him a large old vestment cross and chain to wear as a protection from Delisle's "heathen slaves."

"Jesus, God, no!" screamed Raphael picking up a warm timber and hurling it with such force, it crashed into a damaged wall causing it to crumble and collapse.

He stormed, seething, back to Derk's cottage. He found the injured man's wife bent over him dabbing at his lip with a dripping rag. Their two children ran into another room when they saw Raphael. He shoved the woman aside and yanked Derk up by the front of his bloodied shirt and kneed his gut. Derk slumped forward. Raphael punched him to the floor and leaped upon him, swinging like a mad man with relentless blows to the face. Derk attempted to hit Raphael but he was too drunk to fight back effectively.

"You were to scare them out, that's all!" Raphael snarled. His fury and guilt were in charge of his senses. In the moment, he wanted to kill Derk. He did not hear Mrs. Vandersort run screaming from the cottage. He might never have stopped had Jacques not pulled him off. "For the sake of God, man, what the hell Rafe, this solves nothing!"

Raphael shook off Jacques' grip. "It makes me feel better."

Raphael stood, glaring at Derk who finally spoke after coughing up blood. "Dah storm started dah fire. I jus did nuting to help put it out. Dah fire begin fast."

"Yeah, you were drinking and you kept drinking until you were drunk, you maggot."

"Listen, Raphael," said Phillip. There's more going on than this! Fort Royal is under siege!" He turned to his brother. "I passed George on the road." After Phillip shared his information with them, Raphael and Jacques said they wanted to be a part of the battle even though it meant fighting alongside the British. Phillip offered to stay at Delisle.

Raphael hated pirates more than he hated the British. Pirates had confiscated many a shipment. At least the British could be bribed to take a cut, not the entire cargo.

He leaned down to Derk. "You had better redeem yourself and earn your keep. I'll be paying your wages from now on. Sober up and help Phillip put this place in order while we go to help save the port."

So anxious were they to leave, Jacques and Raphael failed to notice the significance of a larger, newly constructed hut behind the stable. Inside, a shadowy figure wearing a headdress of small skulls and feathers, laughed a deep, nasty laugh of contempt. Her carefully crafted plan had begun easily. The only person who had the knowledge to stop her was too old and not nearly as powerful ...

The men traveled back to Twin Flames to notify Suzonne about the invasion of pirates on the other side of the bay at Fort Royal. Milo said, "Suzonne has gone off with Tumba. He wanted to show her something near the cliff house."

Raphael rode home to fortify his weaponry and speak to his family. His beleaguered wife, Adeline, had recently moved their energetic young sons home from the dark, cavernous safe house. She was ill equipped to keep them occupied for lengths of time when they were home from boarding school. "You're going to fight pirates?" she squealed. "What is to become of us? We have only just survived a hurricane. How dare you leave me to my own devices with Charles suffering his wound and storm damage as far as the eye can see!"

Raphael busied himself gathering powder horns and muskets. "Adeline, don't stir yourself into hysteria. Charles has made progress. You're in no danger here. Lock the doors as you always do. Tumba will keep the slaves busy. I'll return within twenty-four hours."

Their son Charles, bandaged and under Rutah's care, pleaded to go along with his father. "I've never seen a battle. Please, I want to see pirates fighting; please papa."

"No, son. You are not well and you're far too young. I need to know that you are here at home healing, safe with your mother."

Old Solomon saddled fresh horses, and Lutesse packed food for them. In less than one hour, the men were off heading toward the blast of gun fire that had begun to escalate. "At least, we haven't heard cannon," said Jacques.

Tumba picked up the tall, well made walking staff that had belonged to Suzonne's father, Etienne. It had been kept leaning near the cliff house door just as Etienne had left it. The hurricane's winds had thrown it some feet away.

Just then, Milo appeared. Struggling to catch his breath, he sputtered, "Raphael has learned that pirates are attacking Fort Royal. He and other planters have gone to help the garrison. Apparently, the pirates are shipwrecked and need another vessel." He slumped into the wild grasses. "Raphael said we are safe here at Twin Flames. I came to fetch you with the news."

"We are safe perched so high above the beach. The cliff protects us. How did you know where we had gone?" asked Suzonne.

"I saw you walk toward the sea. I know where Tumba prays."

Tumba assisted the winded man to his feet. He motioned for Milo to look over the cliff. When he saw the wreckage, Milo held his hand to his temple dropping the machete he found abandoned in the cane fields along the way. "Oh dear God, Raphael does not know about this!"

"The bell tower rang only once. Do you know why?" asked Suzonne.

Milo paused finding it difficult to concentrate on anything accept the carnage below. "Jerome wanted to be a hero. He overheard Raphael and Jacques speak of the pirates. On his own, he climbed the tower and rang the bell. Raphael ran up there in a fury. I think he feared it might have been one of his sons. "He yelled raw words at Jerome saying he had no need to cause panic; the pirates were in Fort Royal, not here. I have been unsuccessful in my efforts to corral Jerome's impetuous nature. Now, he is to be punished." Milo's black eyes showed his pain.

"Rest Milo and regain your strength before you go back to the plantation. Don't worry. As it happened, Jerome did the right thing ringing the bell tower. I'll make certain Rafe backs down about it. Truthfully, he will be exhausted when he returns from Fort Royal. He won't have any fight left. The pirates were a great ploy for some time away from Adeline."

Milo arched his eyebrows at Suzonne. More and more, she reminded him of her ever progressing maturity.

"I think you know what I'm referring to," she said.

"Suzonne, surely you do not believe your brother would ..."

Suzonne interrupted, "Yes, I do. I don't have my head in the clouds. Camille has heard gossip. Be that as it may, Milo we have more important things to think about than Rafe's indiscretions. We've raised the black flag. Tell Jerome to go back to the bell tower and ring it with abandon! Thank goodness, I have you to help me see to the comfort of Camille and her mother.

"I expect they will require many hours of sleep," said Milo.

"Rutah says sleep is the spirit healing itself. You were good to come all this way to tell me about the invasion. It eases my mind to know that the able bodied pirates are in Fort Royal. Tumba and I are going down on the beach for a closer look."

"Suzonne! You cannot be serious!" cried Milo.

She raised the spyglass to count the bodies lying at every angle on the white sand below. There were thirteen; unlucky thirteen. A shiver shot up her spine. The number thirteen had been considered unlucky in her own Catholic upbringing since the time of the Knights Templar, but in the voodoo practiced by Martinique's slaves, it held dominion.

Most brigantines were large enough to carry a crew of one hundred. How many had this ship carried? How many corpses lay at the bottom of the ocean and would be churned by the currents to float bloated, twice their size along the shore in the weeks to come?

Suzonne saw no long boats or dinghies. She wondered about the number of survivors who had made their way to Fort Royal. None of the bodies on the beach were moving but the glass was not fine enough to detect shallow breathing from her vantage point. Yet, she said, "We have nothing to fear. The only pirates on our land are dead."

"Look for yourself. All that you'll see is a basket of noisy chickens." She thrust the spyglass into Milo's hands.

Milo closed one eye and squinted to focus. He moved the glass slowly over the cove. "I see what you have seen. Yet, my apprehension is no less. You place yourself in the unknown for what purpose?"

"This is the most exciting thing to have happened in my lifetime. It may be my only opportunity to see a real pirate!"

Milo and Tumba appeared stricken. Tumba had hoped Milo could dissuade his mistress. Milo knew Suzonne to be wise beyond her fifteen years, though on more and more occasions she caused him to be frightened for her. Without Etienne to rein in his daughter, Milo had seen her increasingly throw caution to the wind. To her detriment, Suzonne was fearless, head-strong and reckless if she believed in the principle. He cared for her as he would for his own child but Milo had no authority. He could only hope to appeal to her intelligence with reason.

"Young lady, is that wise? You can see everything from here where you are safe. I do not speak from ignorance. As a young man, I spent time amongst pirates. They were barbarians."

Suzonne put down the spy glass. "I've never heard that story. If you choose to share it with me later, I would feel most privileged. Milo, the pirates you experienced were alive. Tumba will be with me. I'm not the least bit concerned. The only living things from that ship on our beach are the chickens. We aren't afraid of chickens are we Tumba?"

Milo and Tumba exchanged glances. Each knew what the other had been thinking; without Raphael to intervene, Suzonne was in charge.

Desperate to stop her, Milo said something he regretted. "Raphael would forbid you to do this!"

Suzonne's rebellion flared. "And where is my brother?" She answered her own question with an icy edge. "He's in Fort Royal playing soldier and visiting an old friend. I could be a part of his adventures if I were his brother instead of a sister. He told me the days of piracy are waning. Captain Renault says there will always be larceny on the open seas. Before they are only stories that old people tell, I want to see a pirate for myself. Come Tumba, we may find treasure," she laughed.

Chapter 8:
Mysteries from the Sea

The hurricane had ripped the disabled ship from the ocean and violently thrust it into the cove. It helplessly rode twenty-five foot swells and came crashing in toward the beach only to break apart on a sand bar. When the hurricane moved inland and the seas calmed, the surviving pirates immediately launched two long boats they were able to salvage from the wreckage.

Under cover of the starless, black night, their calloused hands were a blessing. Having leathered palms enabled them to row the grueling two hours it would take for them to cross the bay. Hungry and exhausted, the pirates slid into the harbor at Fort Royal, unnoticed.

There had been destruction here as well. The storm dislodged an anchor causing two ships to collide. Workman planned to begin repairs at sunrise and the townspeople were certain to be swarming the wharf to watch. More troubling to the pirates was their abandoned brigantine. How soon would it be discovered and reported to the garrison. They had to act quickly and they could ill afford mistakes in judgment. Captain Skaggs depended upon them. No one wanted to suffer the punishing wrath of his anger.

Seventeen pairs of experienced eyes carefully inspected the moored vessels spared by the hurricane. The determined pirates must commandeer a craft built for the greatest speed. They knew the British would pursue them. A newer clipper with sleek lines, flying the white shield flag of Portugal, caught their attention. It had the potential to swiftly spirit them out to sea ahead of any warships. They did not want a large cumbersome cargo ship built for heavy casks of rum and hogsheads of sugar. This vessel, most likely, transported spices and citrus. A perishable cargo necessitated a ship capable of reaching its destination ahead of spoilage. Thus, it had fewer cannon to maintain a weight conducive for speed.

The pirates desperately needed their replacement vessel well stocked with supplies. They watched in the shadows of early dawn as three Portuguese sailors assisted by two roustabouts loaded the ship's holds with several wagons of necessities. It appeared they were preparing to sustain themselves for several weeks of travel and were only waiting the storm's passing.

Six well-armed pirates shinnied up the ropes of the under-protected ship. Most of the crew was being entertained in one of the island's several brothels before setting sail.

A pirate named Tagget, who decided to increase the success of their mission, created a diversion. He set fire to the Blue Fish tavern while the greater number of pirates lurked behind stacked crates or blended in as foreign sailors. All were anticipating their opportunity to scramble on board as soon as the five men loading were subdued.

The first pirate to hit the deck surprised a young Portuguese sailor walking up the gang plank with a load of dried fish. He threw a dagger, hitting the sailor in the shoulder. The Portuguese fell but not before crying out and firing a wild pistol shot. The loud pop alerted the British military patrol. The injured man was shoved off into the harbor by charging pirates as they boarded the ship before the soldiers took positions against them.

The roustabouts escaped but the sleeping captain and the two remaining sailors were taken prisoner and chained on deck for all to see which made it almost impossible for the soldiers to fire. Panic ensued amongst the townspeople when they got word the pirates had turned the ship's cannons to face the city.

The pirates made a spectacle of the cannon, loading and manning them to fire. When the British moved a frigate in an attempt to block the Portuguese vessel from leaving, the fugitives made ready to fire at it. They threatened to sink every vessel surrounding them. To prove it, they lobbed a cannonball at the frigate causing flames on its deck.

Raphael and Jacques were not able to shoot pirates as they had hoped. Instead, they rescued the bar keeper at the Blue Fish by pulling him from his burning establishment. They laid the man near a fountain with a spouting fish.

Raphael ran in back of the building to a brothel he frequented called Crimson Rose. The painted red door was always kept locked. He picked up a large empty rum barrel and used it as a battering ram. The heavy door jamb never gave way but the door itself cracked enough to be kicked-in. A shirtless patron with no shoes shoved past Raphael, holding up his trousers. Two prostitutes in robes followed gulping for air.

Jacques broke down a second door to rescue Fayelynn, the brothel's madam who had stopped breathing. He carried the lifeless woman out and left her in the care of her ladies while he began a water brigade to save the building.

Covering his face with the crook of his arm, Raphael plunged into the black tunnel of smoke that filled the hall. Though he could see nothing, he found her by memory. Nude, she frantically clawed at her warped window. "Scarlett!" He ran and embraced her with his entire being running his hands up and down her back. "I'll get you out!" With danger raging toward them, Raphael found he was unable to tame his heated loins. He never could when near her. He kissed her passionately just before lifting her through the window.

Adolescent boys who had come to see the pirates, whistled, howled and pointed at her. Raphael grabbed Charlotte's valise where she kept her costumes and threw it out the window, after her. "Put something on!" He chased the boys screaming. "Get the hell away you gawking little bastards, or I'll cut off your mangy balls and feed them to the seagulls!"

One of the boys turned around after he had run a safe distance and yelled, "Men pay money for that whore to take off her clothes. We got to see her naked for free!"

Suzonne stood on the cliff looking down at the treacherous venture they faced. She knew the long steep path to the cove involved risk. Nevertheless, it drew her as nothing aside from Rutah's teachings ever had.

Tumba's deep voice became serious. "Mam'selle, I not afraid of rocks or any man. I afraid of dead man spirit. Bad man have bad spirit." Tumba despised every aspect of going below to walk amongst recently departed souls. Even worse, these were immoral strangers whose spirits had been severed from their bodies as their owners met violent deaths.

Suzonne pointed to a cloth pouch Tumba wore tied with sinew about his neck. She knew it held amulets that Rutah had given him. Though he prayed Muslim, voodoo crept into every slave's belief system. He had seen the power of voodoo.

"We can't be harmed from this world or the next. Our powerful gods will accompany us. Your God protects you and I have this." She gestured to her father's gold crucifix. He had placed it into her hand the hour he died.

An apprehensive Tumba was not convinced. "Allah keep me strong from enemies I see."

"I won't force you Tumba. I honor your beliefs but I'm going regardless; with you or without you." Suzonne smiled. She remembered a time when unbeknownst to their parents, she and Camille, as children had climbed down the cliff using the rope. All went smoothly until a gust of wind coupled with a misstep on loose rock had caused the rope to swing-out crashing them into the craggy surfaces. Later, after an afternoon of swimming and looking for pirate treasure, they had made a pact never to tell anyone the true nature of their cuts and bruises.

Tumba knew his responsibility should be watching over the operation of the fields as Raphael would have ordered. Yet, how could he abandon his young mistress who obsessively insisted on placing herself in danger? He saw a defeated looking Milo standing in the shade wringing his hands in silence. Only he, Tumba could shield her from injury or worse. Taking the life of a fellow human had always been against his faith. Would Allah forgive him if the human were a pirate?

He joined Suzonne who had begun unrolling a nautical lanyard as thick as his fist, lowering it down the side of the cliff. It had been secured to a forged spike a yard long buried deeply into the crust of the mountainous terrain. The rope made it possible to navigate the narrow path gradually winding down in serpentine fashion from side to side.

Suzonne used Milo's kerchief to secure her dress at the hem connecting front to back in the center. The alteration transformed her dress into makeshift bloomers. Milo rolled his eyes. "Oh, don't pretend to be shocked." She laughed. "It was you Milo, who conceived the idea. This is the way you dressed Camille and I for our swimming lessons."

Tumba and Suzonne began their decent. He went first to be able to help her if she faltered. He moved with caution, keeping a watchful eye on her progress. The rain-worn path gave way at intervals sending stone and soil hurdling downward crashing, bouncing off previously fallen rocks below.

Clutching the rope with both hands, it required all of Suzonne's strength. How she wished she had worn her leather riding gloves and boots.

The rope slacked. Tumba thumped to the sand. She heard the flapping wings of startled flesh-eating birds of prey. For the first time, she looked down. Tumba had made it safely and she was almost there. He held out his arms for her to jump the final few feet.

They stood unable to move, facing a scene resembling a massacre! It was quite a different thing to view the disaster from the top of the cliff. Now they were within touching and smelling distance. Suzonne willed her eyes to skim over the human remains unable to find the courage to look directly at them. She saw old timbers, rotting food, two dead pigs and a basket of clucking chickens. "How did they survive this horror?" she asked.

"Pigs die. Chickens gift to man from Allah."

This was not the first time Suzonne had seen drowning victims but this ... all this. The stench of garbage and death caused her to cover her nose. The tide chose to deposit the ship's spillage in large heaps of humanity and destruction. Amongst the bodies were baskets, barrels, rough-hewn chests, planks of splintered wood, and weaponry of all types.

The corpse closest to her nearly buckled her knees with a wave of nausea. His mouth was opened wider than humanly possible with flies already swarming in and out. Next to him, the body of a red-haired lad with a sprinkling of freckles across his cheeks bore a frozen look of terror in his dead blue eyes. How had he come to serve on a pirate ship? Did he have a mother searching the horizon praying for his safe return? Had she given him the St. Christopher medal he wore?

Suzonne and Tumba moved from corpse to corpse, stepping over tangled legs and arms. This was not as thrilling as her imagination had painted it. She thought of them as sad, misguided men whose lives had a terrible end. It would be her mission to see that they receive the last rites of the church.

She had expected to see them wearing colorful clothing. In her childhood stories, they were depicted dressed in velvet coats, lace collars, and shiny buckled boots; elaborate things stolen from their victims. Most of these men wore coarse clothing and their faces were scarred and weathered.

Suzonne saw a leather bag secured around the waist of large frightening-looking man. "Give me your dagger, Tumba."

"Mam'selle," he exclaimed in protest. "He dead!"

"I know." She pointed to the bag.

"Ohhh, mam'selle, bad spirits!"

Suzonne felt energized. "If I'm correct, it may contain coins." The sharp dagger freed the bag with ease.

Tumba's face clearly expressed his shocked disappointment in her.

"Do you believe that I'm stealing from the dead, Tumba? Well, I guess I am but for good reason. If I don't take it, the British will confiscate it along with everything else of value. Unless there's another storm to dislodge this wreck, it will never drift ashore. It has run aground and the tides are further swamping it. Weeks will go by before it gives up all its contents. As for me, I'm merely redistributing the stolen spoils of pirates to be used for a wonderful family in great need. I intend to give everything we find to Camille and Madame Delisle in hopes they can rebuild their plantation. See how beautifully both of our gods are working together? I believe your Allah and my Heavenly Father approve of this. Good does triumph over evil."

They found six more bags. One had been fashioned from a stocking. All were filled with what felt like jewelry and coins. Then, protruding from underneath the corpse of a rotund man was a small gilded case. Suzonne might never have seen it had the corner not glittered in the sun.

"Help me turn him over, Tumba."

The giant slave backed away and shook his head. Suzonne shamelessly pushed the corpse over with her foot. Tumba shuddered.

She pulled the object from its hiding place and held it, marveling at the beauty of the decorated presentation case. In the center an elaborate crest of blue and gold inlay had been affixed. What did the case hold? The seal was broken but had been poorly repaired and secured. She dare not take the time to pry it open it now.

She placed the bags and case near the cliff rope while Tumba rescued the noisy chickens from a tide pool.

Suzonne took a last look at the pirates. Many were wearing a single gold circular earring; the price of a Christian burial. She thought these men regardless of their deeds in life, should be humanely buried. "I'll see to it," she promised aloud as if they could hear her.

Chapter 9:
The Man from her Dreams

"Mam'selle, we go?"

"Yes. We must go." Suzonne said. "I need to spend time in the chapel with Adeline and the boys. They're probably there already praying for master Raphael's safe return from the battle as well as the other brave men who are fighting the pirates." In her mind, she knew that In spite of his motives, her brother had placed himself in grave danger.

Suzonne and Tumba walked toward the rope when they were startled by a moan emanating from a body laying face down across a rum barrel. The startled pair stood like statues looking at each other, straining to hear more. Several yards from the others, the man had been disregarded as just another dead pirate ... until now!

Suzonne could no longer tolerate the suspense. She approached the man with Tumba following close behind. "He's breathing! Tumba, help me turn him over!"

"Mam'selle, please no."

Suzonne began tugging at the man's clothing to turn him over by herself when she saw the chain. "He's chained to the barrel. This man is a prisoner. Help me!"

Tumba yanked the chain. The old warped wood began to give way but held. He used a chunk of stone from the cliff to hack the chain until it broke. Now, Tumba was involved. He too, had been a prisoner on a ship. He easily moved the unconscious man from the barrel on to the sand, laying him on his back.

Suzonne gasped, thunderstruck, so stunned, she weaved. Had Tumba not held her shoulders to steady her, she may have fallen. He assisted her to a seated position on the other side of the barrel.

"Mam'selle, sick?"

Suzonne struggled to regain her senses. She looked at the sky, the cliff, and the expanse of ocean fearing she might see rainbow seagulls or mermaids frolicking in the surf which would explain that this man too was an apparition or some kind of magic. She dug her hands in the sand and felt the soft, warm granules sift through her fingers like sugar falling back onto the beach. The sand felt real. Tumba looked real. She had heard Tumba's question. If the sand and Tumba existed, then the man on the beach must not be a phantom.

"Mam'selle?" A confused Tumba felt woefully inadequate. He did not understand why she looked at him so strangely. He worried that bad spirits had done something to his mistress and with Rutah so far away, what should he do?

Suzonne abruptly stood. She had to see that face again! With her heart pounding, and using the barrel for support, she peered over it to stare, transfixed at the most beautiful man she had ever seen! Yet, she had seen him many times. She dreamed about this man. He had monopolized her dreams for many months. Recently, she had begun indulging herself with an afternoon nap every day just to see him again.

Overflowing with emotion Suzonne collapsed beside the man on the sand. In her dreams, she loved him. In her dreams, his black hair curled about his face as it did now. In her dreams, she brushed the curls from his dark eyes. She reached with a trembling hand to do so in this the real world. His forehead felt smooth and warm; his hair damp. Though his eyes were closed, she knew with certainty, their exact shade of brown. He's real. This is not a dream. She heard Tumba speak.

"Man pirate?"

She found her voice. "This man is no pirate. He's dressed like a gentleman." Suzonne noted that his soiled and torn clothes were of the finest quality. The fabric and fashionable workmanship spoke of a genteel lifestyle. These were not the ill-fitting garments worn by pirates. His clothing had been tailored to fit him perfectly.

Suzonne observed that his face had a healthy color though it might be sunburn. His shallow breathing worried her but most concerning of all were the two bloody gashes he sustained on his head. She soaked the hem of her dress with salty sea water. When she dabbed gently at the gash near his temple, he groaned.

Suzonne flinched! "I'm sorry. I'm so sorry." She held his hand and kissed it.

A bewildered Tumba stood mute.

The wounds were no longer bleeding. "I feel I have to clean them the best that I can no matter how he protests." She used Milo's kerchief dipped in surf, then, tied it like a bandage around the man's head.

"This gentleman's wounds need to be properly dressed and he requires much attention. We'll take him home with us. I'll be his caregiver. I know that with Rutah's help, we'll be able to return him to health. I believe it is no accident that he was brought to me."

Tumba only wanted his mistress safely returned to the manor before master Raphael came home. "How we git man home, mam'selle?"

"We will accomplish it with that sail." She pointed to a large length of torn sail sloshing to and fro in the waves.

"Mastah Raphael not like man come to manor. He git Derk black snake after me."

Suzonne's eyes flashed wildly. "They'll be no whipping on Twin Flames, ever! I will defend my father's rule until I breathe my last breath. As long as I'm here Tumba, you need never fear the whip! As for my brother, I'll tell him that I ordered you to do this for me. I will even say you voiced concerns against it."

Tumba pulled the drenched sail fragment across the sand. Together, Suzonne and he lay the injured man on the makeshift sling they had fashioned. They exchanged anxious glances. The tall, fine-featured man in the sling was slender from days of captivity. But, to carry dead weight up the steep, rocky winding incline ...

"Can you do it, Tumba? I know he's heavy."

"Molasses cask more big." He gestured with his arms. Tumba's broad shoulders and arms rippled with his tremendous strength. He slung the encased man, who uttered muffled sighs, over his shoulder.

"Ohhh, be careful," winced Suzonne. "He must suffer pain."

Tumba walked slowly to the cliff rope looking wistfully at the chickens. How he had looked forward to presenting them to his woman. His chest expanded to its capacity as he prepared for the task before him with a deep inhalation of sea air. "Allah, keep me strong, not fall, mam'selle." He began the climb; hoisting himself and his charge up the harrowing cliff. With massive hands of iron, he griped the coarse rope and pulled while trying not to jostle the heavy sail he clutched in his other hand.

Suzonne tied the coin bags about her waist in the same fashion as the pirates. She had already placed the elegant case in the sling beside the former captive.

When Tumba reached the top, his blue-black skin glistened with perspiration. He laid down his burden to help Suzonne. He could not help eyeing the chickens fussing in their basket on the sand below as he assisted her to the summit.

"Go get them Tumba, You've earned a souvenir for your efforts today. Hurry!"

Milo had been watching them from atop the cliff, more afraid for them than they were for themselves. "Suzonne," he erupted with relief,

"I so feared that you might be injured." His smile quickly vanished. "Why have you dragged this pirate up from the wreck?"

She parted the sail to gaze upon the dark haired man checking his condition. Encouraged, she held his wrist to her cheek and she was filled with the giddy anticipation of learning everything about him.

"Pirates are murderous criminals!" cried Milo.

"No, no Milo, this man had been the pirate's prisoner. Tumba broke his chains. He's been injured. I plan to care for him."

"Suzonne! He may bring disease to Twin Flames. You must consider that possibility."

"My work with Rutah serves me well. I see no pox or rashes. I believe he suffers as the result of head injuries and only requires food, drink, and good care." Suzonne did not want to entertain the thought of anything negative. In her mind, Rutah would be able to heal him and when that had been accomplished she will be able to spend time with this beautiful man ... the man from her dreams.

Suzonne swung around to the small rain barrel her father kept to water the bougainvillea brilliantly twining over the cliff house door. She scooped a halved gourd into the fresh storm water to drizzle the lips of the unaware man. He licked the moisture from her fingertips. Even though his eyes never opened, the eager touch of his lips on her fingers sent hot tingles racing through her body. Suzonne smiled as she experienced this provocative new surging flush of emotion.

"Milo, look, he's responding!"

Milo bent closer. "He is not conscious. This man may have the plague."

Suzonne felt the man's forehead again. "We must hurry." She continued to administer to him until Tumba returned from the beach with his chickens.

Tumba held his retrieved souvenir in one hand while his other hand pointed toward Fort Royal. Smoke curled above the small city. Something was ablaze!

Suzonne reached again for the spyglass. From this vantage point, high on the cliff, it was possible to see nearly a mile in each direction. She painstakingly scanned the skyline turning in a half circle as she checked for further signs of trouble. She saw the fire at Fort Royal but it appeared to be isolated in one building. The waterways were nearly clear. Everything looked as it always did after a hurricane. There was nothing obvious to arouse fears of any impending danger. Twin Flames gave every indication of tranquility. Yet, she felt apprehensive, sensing something ...

Though not possible to see it all, Suzonne felt a precautionary need to follow the sloping path back down the cliff with the glass as well. She silently chided herself for having something rare, for her; an uneasy, tight fist of nerves gripped her belly. After all, what did she expect to see? Only the usual viper sunning itself filled the lens.

Tumba and Suzonne began the long descent, each taking a side of the stretcher, mindful to pull it on the grassy side of the rocky path. Milo volunteered to be in charge of the basket of chickens.

This final trek down-hill from the cliff house might have been easier had the threesome not been fatigued from their previous climbs. With the gentleman beginning to emit signs of discomfort, Suzonne felt they dare not pause until they were well into the fields. When they did stop to rest, each mopped their brow in their own way while Suzonne administered to the man.

"Don't despair. We've rescued you from the pirates and soon you will be in my home being treated with the greatest of care. I hope you understand me as I only speak French or English well. If you are Spanish, Milo will be our interpreter. I pray you are French so we may converse with privacy."

Milo and Tumba shared an exasperated expression.

They tugged the hammock-like stretcher along the soft muddy lane toward the manor house. The damaged fields were eerily empty of workers, which was to be expected. The slave quarters and the refinery were located on the other side of the fields and the slaves did not work without an overseer. They were told to take shelter in the refinery when there was a bad storm. Had they emerged after the storm subsided, they would have been too terrified to leave after seeing the black pirate flag flying over the cliff house.

Milo said, "Raphael has a great deal ahead of him when he returns from Fort Royal. He must determine if the cane can be saved and harvested, or burned."

"Burn fields, vipers run out," said Tumba.

Suzonne asked, "Has there been any damage to the green houses.

"Only minor tears to the roof," answered Milo.

Large billowing clouds allowed a few rays of sunshine to stream through, lighting the ravaged fields. The plants were not being whip-sawed by the wind as they had been earlier. Now the frayed giants swayed almost gracefully in the strong breezes that had replaced the wind.

Suzonne knew it might be wishful thinking, but had the fields begun to revive under the suns influence? Perhaps the crop's resilience would save it. She felt encouraged that all might be well when she realized that the familiar fresh scent of the sea mixed with sweet sugar cane had returned.

Only moments apart, the sounds of gunfire increased in the distance and the unconscious man moved and groaned. They put him down. Suzonne touched his forehead with the back of her hand.

"He is feverish!"

Simultaneously, Suzonne and Tumba picked up their ends, pulling faster with an adrenaline-driven urgency working in their favor. The man twitched periodically sending frantic chills of worry down Suzonne's spine. Had he awakened? Was he breathing? She couldn't look at him enough.

Tumba softened his feelings against the sick man as he watched the intense efforts of his mistress to save this person she did not know. The

man needed to be fed. Tumba had seen much suffering in his home
land from starvation and he saw the look of death from dehydration in
the bowels of a slave ship.

"Mam'selle, man not die. He hurt, he hungry, He strong alive."

"Thank you Tumba. I pray so."

They turned their attention to Milo. The winded man had pushing
himself too hard for his age.

"Put down the chickens, Milo. Tumba can get them later."

"Without them, I can go ahead and make a bed ready for the
gentleman," said Milo.

"Yes, if you have the strength without hurting yourself. We'll be
close behind. I ask that you prepare papa's room for him."

She heard Milo gasp his disapproval. "Etienne died in that bed! It
has remained untouched ..."

"I know. It has been untouched for two years. Papa always
advocated for the unfortunate. I feel he would want me to do this. We
have made his apartments a shrine. Papa would be the first to say let the
mourning time be over."

Milo raised his arms to signify a truce as he walked on but he
looked back to say, "I am more concerned about Raphael's temper
toward you if he feels strongly against this decision."

Suzonne shook her head. "I will not ... I cannot allow anyone, not
Rafe, not you, no one to interfere with me and this man. I am meant to
do this."

Milo left the large double entrance doors ajar for them. They put
down the heavy stretcher.

Suzonne sank to the floor. "We accomplished it!" She put her head
to the sick man's heart. She was comforted to hear how strongly it beat.
Tumba leaned on the open door.

"Tumba, are you able to carry him upstairs?"

"Yes, mam'selle. I carry mastah Etienne down. I carry man up."

"You bring back a picture in my mind of a dreadful day. How ironic that papa's room has remained just as he left it to be with mama. Now a stranger has appeared to bring it life again. I know you are capable of carrying him. My concern was do you have the strength for it after all you have had to do this morning?"

Etienne's apartments consisted of a small sitting room, a dressing room and a large corner bedroom. A louvered door led to a long balcony from which a good deal of the plantation could be seen. Suzonne parted the mosquito netting from the tall mahogany bed. She pushed aside the silk quilt and saw that Milo had placed a muslin tablecloth over the fine linens.

She motioned for Tumba to lay the man down. "Gently, gently."

Milo stepped forward.

"Thank you Milo."

He beseeched her. "Are you confident that we have not brought danger into your father's sanctuary?"

Ignoring him, Suzonne set about removing her patient's bloodstained, dirty clothing.

Chapter 10:
Two Strangers in one Day

Milo fretted with the gross impropriety of Suzonne's brazen actions; bringing home this potentially dangerous man and now undressing him! Etienne had asked him to guide and protect his daughter when he left this earth. The task had been easier when his charge was a child. Now that she teetered between adolescence and young womanhood, he worried that he might fail his old friend.

Tumba thought nothing of the kind about his mistress. He and Suzonne often assisted Rutah in the slave quarters attending to injured slaves. He automatically began to help Suzonne by pulling off the man's boots.

"Good, Tumba. I will use all the broth I can get him to accept and flood his body to force out the sickness. In the meantime, the fever will not consume him if I cool him with strips of linen dipped in cold water. Before you go to the cistern, send Fancy for Rutah and ask Lutesse for a pail. Tell her I need hot broth and a pitcher of blended juices."

Tumba ran to the cookhouse while Milo came to her aid as she struggled to take off the man's damp shirt. A shiny gold chain caught the light.

"He wears a locket!" exclaimed Suzonne.

"Open it," said Milo. "You may learn his identity or find a clue regarding his homeland."

As if in protest, the man moaned and his face tightened. Perspiration streamed down his cheeks onto his chest detouring into the circle of curly black hair in the center.

"He suffers so! Why does his fever settle down only to return with greater intensity?" Suzonne asked.

She found a sea sponge in her father's toiletries and dipped it into the soapy bowl of water Milo had left on the table. She sighed happily when her velvet strokes with the sponge calmed him. Then she reverently unfastened the locket's clasp to remove it from his neck. "It's lovely." She held it high to admire it. The locket swung from the chain looped loosely through her fingers. The craftsmanship was finer than anything she had seen in her mother's jewelry wardrobe. "I could never open this without permission, Milo. It wouldn't be proper."

The locket itself boasted an intricate coat of arms. She traced the design with her finger. Something about it seemed familiar. "I'd be most interested in knowing the name of this family."

"Suzonne, you cannot be certain that the gentleman did not steal his clothing, as well as the locket."

"Milo, remember that the pirates kept him chained to a barrel. How could he have been one of them?"

Consumed with skepticism, the kindly man continued his argument. "Might you consider the possibility that he was indeed one of them but chained because he committed an infraction against his fellows? It makes no sense to me that they did not rob him of the locket."

Suzonne answered without hesitation. "He must have hidden the locket under his clothing. Look at his hand. He wears no ring. Yet, on his little finger there is a slight indentation where he had worn a ring for some time. I believe they did rob him of his purse and his ring."

Tumba returned with the pail of cold water in one hand and a stack of linen napkins in the other.

"Rutah and Lutesse come soon."

"How clever of you to think of the napkins."

"Lutesse think of it."

"Milo and I were about to tear some old bed linen into strips. Tumba, get those chickens once and for all take them home to your family."

"Mam'selle?" Tumba eyed the stranger.

"I'm in no danger. He's not strong enough to slap a mosquito. This is your time to rest. When master Raphael returns there will be no rest."

Suzonne set about removing the man's trousers. Milo loudly protested.

"It is not fitting for you to do that. Allow me or Rutah ..."

"No, Milo. This is no time for modesty. He will be in my care. In that regard I'll see everything he has anyway. After all, I must bathe him daily."

Nevertheless, when all the clothing lay in a pile on the floor, Milo quickly covered the naked man's body with a blanket. He looked about the room. "Forgive me, Etienne. The challenges grow stronger while I grow older and weaker."

"You worry for both of us, dear Milo," said Suzonne.

Milo shook his head in frustration and stepped out into the hallway to look down the staircase. "I was able to alert Lutesse before you arrived to prepare food. She will be along soon."

Sabre, could no longer climb the steep stairs. Instead, he whimpered, seated below at the first step.

Suzonne said, "Poor thing, he knows I'm here. His bones hurt worse after a storm. It's torture for him when he can't be near me, but he cries out with pain should anyone attempt to pick him up."

Lutesse entered the room with a tray of fresh baked bread and hot tea. She stared disbelievingly, at the man lying in her former master's four-poster bed.

"The bread is warm and the tea is hot. Please sit and eat something before you are taken ill as well," pleaded Milo to Suzonne. "In that small interval of time Lutesse will return with the broth and juices you requested."

This time Suzonne listened to Milo. Her father's bedside chair beckoned her to sink into it. The bread and tea were just what she needed and she was grateful for it.

As she poured her second cup of tea, Rutah's rattling necklace of charms and the humming of her healing mantra could be heard moving up the stairs. The practitioner, fortified by her spirits, cast discerning eyes past Suzonne and Milo to the visitor she had been able to delay for more than two years.

The spirits had warned Rutah. She must not attempt to stop the natural progression of Suzonne's soul's life lessons. Otherwise, her mistress could suffer dire consequences. Rutah had been only allowed to delay his arrival. She knew the placement of time had the ability to influence eternity. Had he entered Suzonne's life when her father was alive, Etienne would have sensed the danger, driving him away causing his rebellious young daughter to leave with him. Had he entered her life soon after Etienne's death, a grief stricken Suzonne would have been even more vulnerable, sacrificing her future for him.

Rutah acted on the single choice available to her. She had postponed their meeting through the manipulation of circumstances. Now, he was here! Did Suzonne have the maturity to make proper choices?

The healer walked close to him. "Rutah know you be pretty," she said.

"What are you saying, Rutah? Do you know him?"

The slave did not answer her for a few seconds, staring at him, shaking her head, while saying, "Rutah know bout him long time. Spirit say you call him to you."

"How? Is it because I dreamed about him?" Bewildered Suzonne asked, "Is he real?"

"He real, mam'selle." Rutah steadied herself with the arm of a chair as she went into a deeper level of concentration. Her visions revealed that Suzonne must be the master of her fate with this man from now on. Rutah would no longer be able to protect her mistress from him.

She held a rattle by its long handle and shook it in a circle around the man's head before shaking it around the perimeter of the bed. She could not resist clearing negativity from around him. That will not be considered meddling, she decided.

"You don't like him," said Suzonne with alarm. She was depending upon Rutah to help the man from her dreams recover his health.

Though she felt his death might better serve her mistress, Rutah said, "Plantation be smaller if Rutah jus fix sick peoples she like." With that, she began the thorough examination her ethics dictated. Holding her hands one inch above the man's body, the healer moved over the length of his torso and limbs, missing nothing. The method of closing her eyes to sense problem areas was all she needed to do. From time to time her hands stopped and her eyes snapped open to give that spot further scrutiny. All the while, Rutah hummed the non-descriptive melody that was hers alone.

Suzonne anxiously held clasped hands to her chin, watching. She had seen Rutah do this countless times but this time was as crucial for her as that terrible day Rutah examined her father in this same way. Suzonne would never forget the expression on Rutah's face when she softly explained that her father could not be fixed.

Rutah said under her breath, "stupid white doctor."

"What do you see?" asked Suzonne.

"Come." The slave stepped aside pointing to small scars on the man's abdomen.

Suzonne studied them closely. "When I bathed him I saw them. I knew they weren't from battle but they were too new to be from childhood. What are they?"

"Rutah know his trouble before he come. Man sick before. Doctor drain blood, say fix him. Stupid. Stupid. Take blood, river of life. Doctor take blood man need fix him."

Suzonne gasped, "He's been weakened! Will he live?"

Rutah smiled. "Man live after bad doctor. He live good after Rutah fix him."

"Thank the saints for you, Rutah!" Suzonne hugged her for the first time. She held the man's hand and spoke to him excitedly. "Rutah says she can help you."

Rutah laid out three herbal powders in earthen bowls from her bag. "Stir warm water or soup, all he take." She turned over Etienne's hour glass to explain the frequency of the feedings and held up two of her fingers to signify every two hours.

Rutah approved of Suzonne's treatment of the man's head wound. "Take long to fix, mam'selle," she fore warned. Before leaving, the gifted slave tucked an amulet between the layers of the bandages wrapped about the patient's head.

Suzonne called after Rutah to thank her again.

"Pretty Monsieur, more to fix," she replied.

Milo helped Suzonne dress the man. She chose a nightshirt of her father's with an embroidered collar she had sewn herself for his birthday. "Thank you, Milo. Will you spend the afternoon with Camille and Madame DeLisle? I'm needed here and I don't want them neglected."

"Yes, of course. How will I know if you are in need of anything?"

"I will find you or I'll call to Jerome from the balcony. Lutesse will be bringing food."

One by one, Suzonne sent everyone away to be alone with him. She must be there when he awakens. There can be no face but hers to greet him when he opens his eyes for the first time.

Rutah's instructions were simple. Suzonne must slowly fill his stomach drop by drop. As time wore on she felt certain his overall body and face had begun to have a tinge of healthy color. Rutah's comments had given her faith in his future.

She allowed herself to relax. Her mystery man slept so peacefully, she lay her weary head back on the chair and closed her eyes. She fell into an exhausted sleep and she dreamed as she always dreamed, of him.

She stood, dressed in a delicate pale pink gown made of a wispy material not of this world. Tiny, cascading pearl earrings adorned her ears. She walked on bare feet across a silky manicured lawn bordered with perfectly shaped dwarf trees. A full moon had begun to rise in the sky when a tall, slim male figure appeared, approaching her with long confident strides. Incredibly handsome, he greeted her with a brilliant smile. He extended his arms. She longed to run to him, fall into his arms, she loved him. He moved closer, speaking her name. He almost touched her but as always, the dream ended before he reached her.

The dream was so upsetting it awakened Suzonne leaving her feeling desperately lonely. This afternoon she awakened with a smile. The very man lay before her. She had been able to look at him for hours and she had touched him all over! After another feeding, she began to brush his thick black hair while talking to him. "Soon I'll be able to tell you about my dream. Wouldn't it be a gift from heaven if you had a dream about me as well? We will have all the hours in the day to get to know each other and some day you will put your arms around me."

Loud boots sounded on the stairs. Her stomach tumbled. Must she face Raphael so soon? She called out. "Did you roust the pirates?"

She smelled him before she saw him; a stench so foul, it was like that of a rotting corpse. The partly closed door flung open with a crash revealing a tall, filthy pirate! His stringy hair hung limp on his shoulders, his cutlass in hand, fresh bright red blood dripping from the blade.

<u>Read The Next Volume:</u>

In the continuing saga
Suzonne of Twin Flames - Volume 2 of 7
By Janie Lynn Peterson
Tell a Friend - Follow Janie Lynn Peterson on Facebook
https://www.facebook.com/JanieLynnPeterson

Don't miss out!

Visit the website below and you can sign up to receive emails whenever Janie Lynn Peterson publishes a new book. There's no charge and no obligation.

https://books2read.com/r/B-A-QPNX-PYAHC

BOOKS 2 READ

Connecting independent readers to independent writers.

About the Author

I always believed that I would write a book. Story-lines flashed through my mind even as a child walking home from grade school on a frigid winter afternoon. I remembered the beauty of a newly fallen snow and it triggered my imagination to create stories about the neighborhoods I passed. In no time, I'd be home having entertained myself all the way.

My sister reminded me that instead of reading stories to her when I babysat, I would make up stories. She never forgot the one about a young dancer who yearned for red ballet slippers but her family had no money.

I rarely recorded my stories. When I did jot down an intriguing few paragraphs, there was no follow through. I saved my notes and moved on to a new interest.

Suzonne of Twin Flames did not allow that. Scenes and dialog filled my brain.

When I didn't write it down, it continued to repeat until I did. However, there was a time limit. If after many opportunities, I had to write it down or run the risk of loosing it. It may or may not repeat weeks later.

I could be driving down a highway with this unrelenting story having a field day in my thoughts.

There were times when I pulled over to write as much as possible on a scrap of paper that happened to be in the console. Eventually I kept a spiral notebook on the passenger seat. I learned to take it everywhere: waiting rooms, shopping, the beach. I never knew when I would be given a thought that had to be captured.

Many times I wrote the chapters until the wee hours, 3 or 4 AM. The next day after reading what I had written I said, "I wrote that? It's really good!"